The Shaman's Child

Heather Wood Ion

The Shaman's Child

The Shaman's Child

Copyright © 2014 Heather Wood Ion

All rights reserved. No part of this publication may be reproduced, distributed, or transmitted in any form or by any means, or stored in a database or retrieval
system, without the prior written permission of the copyright holder.

10 9 8 7 6 5 4 3 2 1

ISBN 978-0-9898056-2-9

Cover design by Nicholas Ion

Text layout by Peter Ion

Requests for permission should be directed to
lilascribe@gmail.com

Heather Wood Ion

Dedication

To those who heal and those who give care,
and in gratitude to all my teachers.

The Shaman's Child

Author's Note

The annual renewal ceremonies of indigenous peoples around the globe remind us to celebrate what we learn as we live. The tribes of the plains of North America were deliberate in teaching their traditions across the generations.

George K. Park, a social anthropologist of imagination and deep humanity, guided the research on which this tale is based. Although that was long ago and far away, I remain constantly thankful that he has been my teacher. Professor Milos Mladenovic at McGill University conveyed vividly and with inspiring humility that history is only understood through story. Jonas Salk was both generous and rigorous as he taught me to seek the unity between science and art in all forms of healing. My father's knowledge and love of the nature of Alberta, and his respect for the native peoples, filled our childhood with wonder and with reverence. To them, and to all of my other teachers, I remain profoundly grateful.

For the liberties taken, I ask forgiveness: the errors are mine, but so too is the love.

San Diego, 2014

The Shaman's Child

Chapter 1

CHAPTER 1

High at the north end of the Great Plains where the tide of the prairie breaks in waves against the mountains, there was once a tribe in which everyone believed in magic. Everyone, that is, except Peewit.

The chief of the band was Peewit's grandfather and he had long white hair, sharp black eyes, and a beaky nose; everyone knew—even before he moved or spoke—that he was the best and most powerful of all the medicine men. His wife had died before Peewit was born, so the grandfather lived in the same tent as Peewit, which made life crowded, and sometimes, strange.

Peewit's father was the best linguist among the medicine tribe, and his mother was the best herbalist, and everywhere there was an aunt or a cousin or an older brother or sister who was the best at something. It was tiresome for Peewit to be merely the youngest.

The woodland Cree had moved to the west and north along the edge of the prairies and mountains. They were always curious to learn. With their songs they were able to soothe even the worst sorrows of winter. Whenever there was a battle among other tribes, a Cree medicine man would be sent to attend the wounded, and often, through his gift with language, he would negotiate a peace between the warriors.

Peewit was five, the very youngest grandchild of the chief. He already knew it was much harder to make and keep peace than to go to war, and he knew that the singers of his family caused the tall warriors of other nations to sit wide-eyed, listening.

Peewit watched everything he could with his whole attention. He was so good at watching by the time he was five, that the tribe had forgotten his name was Peewit. They called him instead Fix-It-Find-It because this little boy who watched could also remember. He knew where someone had put down a favorite needle when someone turned to stir a pot of stew.

Because they were all so good at everything, the cousins and uncles and brothers and sisters took for granted that Peewit was good at fixing and finding things. Peewit felt himself the disgrace of his family because he thought fixing and finding was not special like singing, or healing. He feared that he caused the family much worry just because he was different. The worry was like a great searching cloud of mist which followed Peewit, even in his sleep. Whenever he could, he would slip away up a tree or into the grasses at the edge of a slough and he would find comfort in watching the ways of the birds and the insects.

Once in a great while when Peewit's grandfather would find him, and sitting cross-legged, he would hold the small boy against his chest and softly ask "What do you see, Peewit?"

Peewit would tell him, exactly. Sometimes it would be of the life

Chapter 1

within a leaf as the sun shone through it, sometimes it would be of the pattern of the bees as they sought and sang of the treasure they found in meadow flowers. As he sat against his grandfather, Peewit felt no shame, but delight in sharing what he saw.

He could talk of the orioles and how they weaved soft lichen and hair into the pouch which cradled their eggs. He could talk of spiders in the earth and how they trapped food. On clear days he could tell of the clouds and the different colors of the sky and what messages the wind was sending. In the winter, whispering so that he did not wake his parents, Peewit would tell his grandfather about stretching skins and beams of the tent as the snow and ice became a burden.

For the grandfather these were times when he would smile to himself, he would always kiss the top of Peewit's head when they parted. Peewit stored these moments within himself as nourishment.

Each year, at the time of the summer solstice, when the earth seemed to pause beneath the sun, the peoples of the plains would celebrate with gatherings and ceremonies. They praised the plentiful food and the earth's abundance. All the medicine men and women competed to show the skills they had learned.

As soon as the evenings were warm enough to sit out beneath the stars, the tribe would practice their songs and dances. Peewit would watch. It was not a time when he could watch for long, for someone would shout "Fix-It Find-It, where is my pipe?" or perhaps a fan of feathers. Peewit would run and fetch whatever was needed as quickly as he could, for he hated to miss any of the practice. He wanted to see how a slow hand waving in smoke could suddenly hold a bird's egg, or how a pot of boiling water erupted into purple smoke.

The Shaman's Child

Peewit had learned that when he paid careful attention, all the details would make sense. But, if he did not pay attention, then whatever he was watching would seem to be a trick, or magic. His older sisters were always very solemn. They sang and scolded Peewit to be very still while they called the spirits to aid them. However, no matter how hard he watched Peewit never saw a spirit. The older he grew the more it worried him that he alone, of all his tribe, could not see those things called spirits. In his sixth summer, Peewit's sisters began to tease him as 'the boy who does not see visions'. In a tribe of seekers, this was not a funny joke for it meant they felt that Peewit was blind in the ways most important to his people.

For Peewit, that summer's festival was the most wonderful there had ever been. His grandfather was acclaimed the best medicine man of all the tribes. Early in the spring, the chief travelled south to the lands of Arapaho peoples. In that land there was tumbleweed instead of clumps of willow and the mountains were a far-off haze. His grandfather, and Peewit's father as well as others of their tribe had gone to negotiate for hunting rights in the Arapaho territory.

Peewit watched them go with great sadness. Now he would be sleeping alone during the cold spring nights. His kindly grandfather's voice would not be there to ask him what he saw. At first, to escape his sorrows, he hid away from the camp, and watched the water birds dance, mate and build their nests. He followed a doe until she felt safe and gave birth to her fawn. He learned hiding was lonely. Fix-it-Find-it was much in demand by the women—everywhere he went they called to him.

"Find me some milkweed."

"I need water lily bulbs."

Chapter 1

"Are the twinflowers out?"

The questions felt like commands to Peewit. They never seemed to stop even as spring turned to summer. Lookouts were sent to the high hills to watch for the return of the chief. The camp had moved to a high valley where Peewit delighted in the new varieties of birds and plants. Sometimes his mother would accompany him into the woods, teaching him the names and the uses of all that they collected. But Peewit gave up asking her the most important question: "Why must this plant work one way and that plant work another?"

When she said "It is the spirit of the plant" and Peewit felt empty as if he had not eaten a meal.

Newcomers arrived and there was much visiting back and forth among the families as they prepared for the ceremonies. Peewit went deep into the woodlands and high on the foothills to find all the roots, bark and moss that the visitors demanded. At night he tried to stay awake to listen to the songs and the tales being practiced, but instead he slept and dreamt of the ceremony to come.

One day his mother spoke sharply to his older sisters and that day Peewit knew something would be different. When the sun was high and his mother's temper had subdued them, Peewit saw a small procession coming from one of the new camps. There were no horses, so it could not be his grandfather. Peewit did not run to greet the visitors. He squatted in the shadow beside the tent where he could watch his mother waiting. Her eyes were tight with expectation.

As the strangers grew nearer Peewit saw that many of them were as young as his brothers and sisters, and he was surprised to see his own siblings run forward. The children with the strangers ran to greet them. A wrestling, racing tumble of cousins slowed the progress of the elders. Peewit glanced to see if his mother was eager, but her mouth was now as tight as her eyes and he wondered who caused this strain. As soon as the adults reached the camp there were cries, like songs, bursting with welcome. Peewit caught a glimpse of a small, plump figure, with the same glowing white hair as his grandfather almost hidden behind the taller young people. He heard his mother sigh and turned to watch, in astonishment, as she ran forward weeping into the arms of a strange woman. He saw that everyone wanted to pat and embrace the pair, so Peewit wandered off.

He found a rotting log at the edge of the camp and to make a map in his head, he followed ants carrying bits of the wood. In another part of the log Peewit thought there might be honey, as he watched bees returning to a tunnel in the log. He was counting, measuring the time between the bees returning, when he heard a shrill call "Fix-it-Find-it come quickly". Reluctantly Peewit trotted back to his mother's tent.

"Is this my sister's youngest grandson? What do you fix and what do you find that you must be called by skills, Child?" The plump woman had eyes full of challenge and her face was as lined as the flesh of an old mushroom. Peewit's mother did not come to the aid of her son.

"Speak up, speak up, or has my brother-in-law made a magic on your tongue?"

As the old woman laughed, Peewit stared for he had never heard anyone joke about his grandfather's skills. Finally one of his older sisters spoke up.

"He fixes anything to do with making things, and finds all that we

Chapter 1

need, the roots and the nests and even the paths of insects. But alas, he sees no visions."

"Come boy, you are strong, are you afraid to have visions?"

Peewit said nothing, he was noticing that this woman had strange designs in the beadwork at her neck, and there were deep colors of red and orange in her skirt. How had she made these colors so bright, for this was not the time of year when berries were used as dye? He wondered to himself and finally met her eyes. She was waiting, but not insisting, for an answer.

"No," he said, "I am not afraid."

"Well then, do you say prayers to welcome the spirits so that they will want to visit you?" The old one held her head to one side, like a nuthatch waiting to pounce, he thought.

"To which spirits, please?" he asked.

It would never do, with his mother and his sisters listening, to be caught and blamed as foolish before a guest.

"Well done, Child, your grandfather would have asked just that question. Let us not hold any examinations now. I am hungry, which at my age is a privilege. Go off and find me the lining of a wood duck's nest while I eat."

Peewit ran off, glad that this stranger did not embarrass him. None of the other children followed him. Peewit loved finding his way in the tangles of dead falls, discovering a new nest, or a different tracery of insects. He moved slowly, listening to the leaves. He examined the changes in the plants, the maturing of the fungi on a tree, the faint hint of ripening in hard green berries. Whenever something interested him, Peewit sat and watched.

At the edge of a small lake, he lay on the warm moss and saw the midday heat shimmer across the water. A muskrat came and decided the boy could be safely ignored. As the animal foraged in the reeds, Peewit watched as a family of ducks moved into deeper shadows. The young were barely smaller than the parent bird. Above Peewit a flicker called in discovery before its hungry thrumming against a hollow tree dominated the woods.

Peewit began to move back to where an old spruce had fallen against another. There the wood duck had nested in the spring. He found a place where he could watch the entrance of the nest and, measuring the shadows as they dappled the forest, he watched until he was sure it was empty. He did not sleep or dose as others did in the midday, but stayed alert to every wasp and movement near the hollow tree.

When at last he was sure he would not disturb any ducklings, Peewit climbed carefully. At last he was able to reach in to the nest hole. He made sure his shirt was secured at his waist, so now he had a carrying pouch. Gently, he pulled the soft down lining of the upper nest away from the wood. When he had as much as he could find that was clean, taking care to leave the bottom of the nest, he climbed down again. He turned back through the forest, gathering tasty berries and mushrooms, knowing they would help fill the pots for so many guests. When he reached the camp, it was filled with the stillness of the gossip which follows after a meal. Not even the dogs raised their heads as he passed. He slipped past his sisters and squatted near the strange woman. When she turned in her talk to laugh at herself she was startled by him.

Chapter 1

"So, Fix-it Find-it, you are a silent stalker as well? Did you find the wood duck's nest?"

"Yes, where do you wish me to put the down?" he asked, and he showed her the handful of the feathers watching as they twisted and turned upon his hand.

"Lay it in a basket with a cover. Do you know who I am?

"You called my grandfather your brother-in-law," he answered.

"Yes, his wife was my sister, but that is not what I meant. What is taking place now that all are gathering and your mother is so nervous?"

"This is the gathering, when all who are already shaman compete and seek students, it is called the Midewiwin."

"Yes, and I shall compete against your grandfather."

Peewit stared in surprise, for there was never any competition against his grandfather, at least that he could remember.

"Do not be afraid, I do not compete for his love for you. We are both great in skills, and it is time that one of us was known as the best of all." She laughed and Peewit shivered, but he asked

"How can there be best when each is different and must be so?"

The old woman laughed and reached out to lean on the boy.

The Shaman's Child

"Tell me, will you tell your grandfather when he comes that you found the wood duck's nest for me?"

"If he asks me, of course."

"You would not keep it secret for me?"

"No, I cannot keep secrets."

"Why not, since you are not a talker?"

"If I try to keep something secret, it clouds my attention and I cannot watch."

"Well I will not burden you, but I wish that your grandfather did not know that I have used your skill."

The new visitors departed and Peewit's mother wearily began to clean the camp.

"Why does she wish grandfather not to know?"

"She is very proud of her skills and many find her frightening."

"People do not find you frightening."

"No, I am a maker of medicines, and a worshipper of plants. There can only be comfort and peace within such medicines if they are to work. You will see many come to the gathering who wish to cause fear for they think that gives them power over the minds of others, even more than the power of the warriors."

Chapter 1

"Is that true?"

"I do not know because those are not my visions."

"But warriors cause death; a true shaman can heal and give more life, why should anyone fear that?

"Your questions must wait for your grandfather. Run see if there is any dust against the sunset. They should be returning."

By the time Peewit reached the crest of the hills the land was deeply shadowed beneath the scarlet of the evening sky. He sat on an outcrop and calmed his breathing as his grandfather had taught him before looking to the glittering rim of the world. After a long time of looking at the light and the patterns the growing darkness made, Peewit decided there was a plume of dust to the far southwest. It was far too big and scattered to be just the small band led by his grandfather. He reported to his mother.

"There is only one strange cloud to the southwest, more than a day's journey, I think. If it is dust, it is made by the dragging of a stretcher behind a horse, a travois, and they travel broadly out of each other's way. If it is smoke, it is a grass fire which jumps and goes out quickly."

"And if it is a spirit come to visit you at last?" teased one of Peewit's older sisters.

"Hush now let him be, he is tired by the visitors."

"Weren't you frightened by the test set for you by our Aunt?"

"What test?"

The Shaman's Child

"When she challenged you to bring her the wood duck's nest, I think it was a test."

"That is no test that is the same as Mother asking me to bring puffballs."

Peewit's sister could not catch him and he vanished, running to the ponies.

"He's too young to know how great our Aunt is, but I thought she was full of power and she was testing him," declared his sister, but Peewit's mother ignored her and soon they all slept.

Chapter II

Peewit was finishing his chores when he heard the camp dogs happily barking, and knew his grandfather had returned. He ran as fast as he could and joined all the women and children rushing and shouting. Peewit's oldest brother stood sweating after his hard ride as the advance messenger.

In one glance, the boy understood that the journey had been a great success, for his brother stood proudly as he talked. Peewit did not wait to hear the report but fetched a water skin and ran out through the camp. As soon as he had reached the high hill, he could see the plume of the dust made by many travelers coming to the ceremony. He found a clear spring and filled the skin with the cold water. He told himself someday he would see the mountains where the spring began.

Unsteady with his burden, he went down to the cleft in the hills where he knew the travelers must pass. Ahead of him, on the trail he could see one of his uncles walking, leading his horse, and clearing the trail of boulders and brush. The men who first passed the boy smiled, but they were strangers and did not ask for the water. Peewit was puzzled, wondering why his grandfather rode at the back instead

The Shaman's Child

of in the front.

"Well Done, Child, it is harsh on the throat to ride behind others all day." Peewit's father rode his horse with ease; his face was in the shadows above Peewit. The boy was reluctant to give anyone but his grandfather the first drink of the spring's water and searched his father's face to learn if he wanted water first.

"It is all right, Son, I will drink after my Father, I am glad to see you."

"Did you gain the hunting rights, Father?" Peewit asked to cover his embarrassment.

"Yes and much knowledge besides. We bring with us a medicine man of the Arapaho who is dying, but he wishes to see our festival."

"Is that my grandson? Peewit?" the laughing voice called from the shadows and dust. Peewit ran forward holding the water high and his grandfather caught him and swung him up in front of him on the pony. After drinking, his grandfather passed the water back to the woman walking beside the travois. She held it for the shriveled man whose eyes glittered at Peewit. He said something.

"He says thank you for the effort you made to bring us cold spring water," translated Peewit's father.

"I hope it gives him comfort and strength," said the little boy as he leaned against his grandfather and realized how much he had missed him.

They moved through the canyon and were soon surrounded by a confusion of children and dogs and the sounds of excitement as each man

Chapter II

left the caravan to join his family. It took most of the day to settle the strangers and Peewit's parents were busy and distracted. Peewit's brothers and sisters unpacked all the bundles, bickering over where this or that should be placed. His grandfather turned this way and that as all who had stored up their troubles asked for his attention.

Peewit took a basket and went into the high woodlands, returning in the afternoon with mushrooms and berries and sweet grasses for a pillow. In the evening, his mother fussed with the meal and chatted in her happiness.

"Yesterday, my Aunt came from their camp; they have journeyed since the last frosts to reach us."

"And is she ready for the contest?" chuckled the grandfather.

"Eager, I think," said Peewit's mother.

"She set Fix-it Find-it a test when we told her he saw no visions," said his sister. Peewit felt his grandfather stiffen as he asked "What was the test?"

"She told him to fetch the lining of the wood duck's nest, but I think it was so that he would meet the wood duck's spirit," his sister said with authority.

"Ah, a wood duck? And did you pass the test, my little Peewit?"

"I do not think it was a test except that she asked if I would keep it secret."

"What did you tell her?"

"That I cannot keep things closed up within my head, because doing that clouds the ways I can see the world."

"And was she angry?"

"I do not know, Grandfather, I do not understand. My mother says that our Aunt wishes others to fear her? How can she be a healer and bring things right if there is fear?"

"It is not given to me to see inside the wishes of any other. I can only tell you what I understand from their actions. Some people act as if what they have is what matters; some people act as if what they do is what matters. Your Aunt is one of the first kinds your mother, father and I are of the second. Therefore, for your Aunt, she thinks her own secrets matter a great deal. I also cannot know if she thinks of herself as a healer or as one who brings things to right. Those who think that healers are able to influence hidden things sometimes do not try to understand what we do, and sometimes that sets us apart and they fear us."

"You mean when we enter a strange camp and all are silent as you pass by?"

"Yes, sometimes, but I also mean the costumes and the paint and the heavy smelling smoke which you remember from other gatherings. All those things create a separation and keep us distant, even from those we try to help."

"But you do not wear the buffalo horns, nor does my mother when she goes to heal."

"No, but your Aunt does."

Chapter II

"It is not the wearing of the horns or the paint or the smoke which makes things right."

"No, Peewit, it is not."

The talk of the evening flowed around them. Just as the grandfather was beginning to sleep, Peewit asked another question.

"Why does my sister, and the others, think that the Aunt would test me because I do not see the spirits?"

"What is it you would want to know if you do see the spirit of a wood duck?"

Peewit turned and looked into his grandfather's eyes.

"Why, how it works, and what it does, and what part of it is what the wood duck is and how it is related to all other things?"

"Anything more?"

"I am sure I would have more to ask once I met a spirit."

The grandfather laughed.

"I am sure you would as well, and I hope that you would ask it. You see, Peewit, you are curious to know things as they are. You do not wish to have them as your own, and you do not ask only what you can use and pretend is yours."

"But why would my sister think Aunt would test me?"

The Shaman's Child

"Perhaps your sister is puzzled that you are so different in the ways you fix things and find things, as you are puzzled by the fears in other people."

Peewit was quiet for a while.

"Grandfather?"

Yes, Child?"

"I am very glad that you are here, but will I ever understand?"

"Is it too much?"

"Yes, sometimes."

"Then let us sleep. I am glad to be back and to have you again beside me."

In the next days, many strangers arrived for the great festival. Peewit rarely went exploring with other boys. More things than he had known had been lost and more things were needed from the forest. In the evening after his chores, he would crouch wearily beside his father who talked with the Arapaho medicine man. Peewit was fascinated by this stranger, and he knew, by the transparency of his skin, that the old man was very sick. Yet his eyes lit with delight and liveliness whenever the little boy stopped by. Sometimes his father would translate Peewit's questions, but more often he would not and would ask the boy afterward how much he had understood.

It was not long before Peewit could imitate his father in the words of greeting and one evening as he returned from the hills, he saw

Chapter II

the Arapaho and his wife alone before their tent, Peewit stopped and shyly spoke the strange words. The frail man beamed and said "I wish you peace this evening," in Peewit's own tongue. With the conversation of eyes and a few words, the boy understood that if he spoke slowly, the old man could understand, just as he could now understand most of what was said.

He showed his snares, and the pouch of items collected for the members of the many medicine societies. Young and old heads bent to examine each item. Peewit told where he had found each, why it was in that specific place, and the old man told him how he would use the ferns or fungus. It was full dark when one of Peewit's older brothers came and irritably told Peewit that he would get no supper for being so late.

With great care, Peewit packed everything into the mosses and placed them in his pouch. He was reluctant to say good-night to the stranger. The old man's hands trembled as he drew the boy to him and hung around his neck the bone whistle which he had worn. Peewit felt the ebbing energy in the old hands, and recognized their blessing. He was lonely when he lay down to sleep after his scolding. His grandfather was somewhere away meeting with the other teachers and Peewit found it hard to sleep alone that night.

Work for the ceremonies had now begun on the sweat houses and the lodges. Peewit ran from his mother's requests to his father's and was scolded by his brothers for laziness whenever he paused. At night sometimes, he would wake hearing the flutes and drums and the soft voices of those who watched the stars. Once, deep in sleep, he felt his grandfather draw him close under the blanket and knew that their breathing matched. His sisters and mother were noisy in their dreams.

The Shaman's Child

In the morning his sister asked if the strange Aunt could put curses upon their sleep. As his grandfather hurried away, he called back "Only if you invite her to do it and let your attention to your fears invade your dreams." She and Peewit argued over their tasks until their mother banished them, sending Peewit off to the higher hills to watch for the last families expected at the gathering.

As usual he was soothed by the forest, and surprised only two competitors practicing in the shadows. The higher he climbed the less he thought about the confusion of his many tasks and the more he thought about his Arapaho friend. Each morning the pains of the night had etched more crevasses upon the old man's face, yet it seemed to Peewit that each morning his eyes were brighter and that he laughed more easily. Peewit knew this even if he only had time to wave as he ran by doing another errand.

As he thought of the dying man, Peewit wondered if the link between them was their shared curiosity. The old man was just as attentive to details as Peewit knew himself to be. He wanted to ask if the Arapaho had ever been called Fix-it Find it? His hand curled around the bone whistle and as he watched the horizon he gently blew into it.

He dropped the whistle in surprise. The sound was like no whistle he had ever heard, but a piercing wail like that of a lonely bird seeking its mate. Peewit tried again, barely breathing into the bone. This time the note was grief itself, and Peewit rubbed away the tears that sprang from his eyes. In his distress he blew harder, and the whistle screamed of pain and anguish and anger. Peewit remembered the only warrior he had seen die after a fight. The day passed unnoticed as he explored all the sounds he could now make. He tried to remember the sounds of other flutes and of the migrating birds crying along their routes.

Chapter II

When he became aware of his thirst, he looked down across the plains and was astonished to see not one but three plumes of dust. He found a stream and drank and began his journey home. He slid on the scree and in haste misjudged and cut himself when he fell. But his message was more important than the blood on his leg, and he delivered it many times, coming at last to his father at the great lodge.

As the men hurried to ride to greet the strangers, Peewit limped away. The Arapaho beckoned to the boy and Peewit let the old hands bathe his cut, pick out the stone fragments with a quill, and then bind up his leg with soft lichen beneath the leather. As he worked, the old man hummed a gentle melody, almost a lullaby. Peewit did not know enough words to ask the questions he longed to ask, so he pulled the whistle out from his shirt and tried to imitate the old man's humming. Then he looked at the old man's face, asking his question with his eyes.

There were tears falling into the man's face, and he nodded at Peewit before he put the whistle back against the boy's chest and pressed his hands there. Peewit's mother was in a frenzy of cooking and did not notice the limp or the bandage as she sent him out with yet another task. After the evening meal was over, his oldest sister said

"Fix-it Find-it, are you a healer so young? That is a very neat bandage."

At once his youngest sister asked if it had been made by the Aunt, she was quiet as Peewit told of the Arapaho's care. His mother sent him off to bed and he heard her talking quietly with his father. This was one of the nights of the vigil when his grandfather did not come to sleep.

The Shaman's Child

In the morning he took a cousin up to the trap lines, and when they returned, the drums for the testing and the ceremonies had already begun.

"Quick, Boy, where is a medicine rattle, I've lost mine."

Peewit remembered that this first procession was for the young apprentices who sought a teacher and to become new members of the medicine society. By the time he had found the rattle, repaired a drum, and improvised a new drumstick, the procession was almost over and he had to wiggle amongst the feet of the watchers to see the assembly before the ceremonial lodge.

His grandfather and the Aunt stood side by side among the other elders of the society. Peewit could see his grandfather was laughing, so he knew the ceremony must be over. The young seekers who would go off on quests stood together in a quiet group, the new apprentices fussed with rattles and feathers, each looking to see how the other was dressed for the long initiation.

Once again, the steady drumming began and when it did the three groups separated: the young seekers turning to the sweat lodges, the apprentices gathering in a circle to sing, and the medicine society entering the ceremonial lodge. Peewit knew that they were still making preparations, and the talk would be a quiet discussion of what each had learned and their recent experiences. He was surprised when one of the Arapaho women asked if they were making secret spells.

"No, they are healers, they do not make spells," he said, but before she could ask him to explain his mother called and sent him asking who needed what in the next four days when there would be no foraging.

Chapter II

That evening grandfather joined them for the meal.

"Grandfather, how soon will the Arapaho healer die?"

"I do not know, but he lives because he wishes to, not because his body gives him more strength.'

"Yes, I see that in his eyes."

"Are you friends?"

"Yes, I hope so."

"He told me you play a medicine whistle."

"He gave it to me, it makes many sounds."

"He has asked that when we take his body to the platform in the trees, you play his whistle for his spirit. Can you do that?"

"I can if you will be there."

"It is a special gift."

"I know," said Peewit sleepily. Soon his grandfather tucked a robe around the sleeping boy. Peewit's mother looked at him with worried eyes.

"He is too lonely for a boy. He does not play as the others."

"Do not worry, he walks his own path. This is not a lonely time for him. That will come later."

The Shaman's Child

"You do not comfort me."

"Think of him with your healer's mind, not as the other boys."

"Shall I ask him to join in the Chicken Dance?"

"Surely, but do not be surprised if he surprises you."

"The Arapaho cleaned his wound, which I did not notice."

"Have you thought that Peewit did not want you to notice?"

"Can a boy of only six summers direct his mother's eyes?"

"How many times have your brothers and other sons directed your eyes away from their mischief?"

She laughed at last.

"You are good for me. Tell me of the talk from those who have come from far. Is there really war again?"

"There is something which is not like the things we know. There are tales of dead bodies with holes in them, right through bone. And there are tales of a new tribe that ask for furs beyond what they wear. They pay for the furs with a drink which paralyzes the drinker so that he cannot move or think well afterward."

"Is it something we know, jimson weed?"

"No, these new traders carry the poison with them. The news is that they are far to the east."

Chapter II

"Will we go south soon?"

"I think we will not go beyond the Blackfoot lands, but stay closer to the mountains."

"It would be good to be near the coal country during the cold."

"I must see if our Arapaho friend is resting."

"Death is very near."

"Yes, but he wants to see the rites."

"Fix-it Find-it spends evenings with him."

"It is good for them both. Perhaps if I tell him our Peewit will dance the Chicken dance he will sleep well."

The Shaman's Child

Chapter III

Chapter III

Long before the dawn, the bands were awake to listen to the chiefs direct the young spirit seekers about their challenge. The youths would go far south, even to the Black Hills or other sacred places, in order to fast and seek a sense of guardian. Before dawn each would go alone away from camps and trails.

Peewit thought the Aunt looked very funny beneath the buffalo horn headdress as she told them "Go and find power within the land, wind or sky and make it your own before you return."

He liked better what his grandfather said, standing in the breeze, his white hair blowing like a banner behind him: "Take with you all that you need from our example and our courage, and from all those who once taught us, you will return cleansed and united with all that we see and all that we know."

Yes, he thought as he bathed, they had almost said the same thing. But he could not ask anyone for once again his mother asked him to find more feathers for the many costumes. She asked if he would join the boys in the Chicken Dance when the sacred time was over.

The Shaman's Child

"Does that mean I can play the hand games too?"

"If the older boys do not object."

"Then, yes, I will dance."

"I do not have freshly dyed feathers, but I believe those worn by your brother are still secure in its sewing."

Peewit made time to examine the costume carefully and found fresh—not dyed—feathers to fill in the tail and wing pieces. His mother lamented that it was all faded to the ordinary browns of the prairie chicken, but Peewit said that was as it should be.

He walked with the Arapaho as they carried the medicine man to watch the procession of the society to begin the sacred time. To his surprise the Arapaho woman offered to help him with the sewing of his new feathers. Many women were busy sewing costumes. The crowd was quiet, waiting.

The first to come was the new leader of the medicine society, from a band which hunted far to the east. As he moved forward the drums began, they would not change their steady beat for many hours.

"He is afraid," said the Arapaho woman.

"No," said Peewit, "He does not want to disappoint; it is the first time he leads." Peewit squirmed, thinking of how he longed sometimes not to disappoint his family, but worried because he did not see visions and thus, he could not say he did.

The initiates from the previous year, the lowest of the degrees of

Chapter III

medicine, came first. Peewit saw one of his sisters and her husband, and several cousins, all shy as they walked to the lodge, chanting. Each wore distinctive insignia proudly, each grade of skills walked separately. Peewit liked the medicine rattles which softened the chanting. In every group there was someone familiar to him and he thought about a society that was sacred, but made of ordinary people.

Peewit noted all the variations of the costumes as if they were plumage on unfamiliar birds; he wondered at the patterns of the quillwork and the vibrancy of the dyes. When his mother passed in the group of the plant healers he knew that all her tension of the past weeks was gone, and now she had given herself to the renewal of the time with her peers. His father's eyes flashed as his mother passed, and Peewit was reassured. As the final ranks of the society moved forward there were fewer and fewer members. Peewit asked the Arapaho how many other festivals there were in lands that he had never seen.

"We peoples of the plains are very scattered, Peewit, so think that this great gathering represents many bands who wander their hunting territories like seed before a wind. How many seeds does it take to make a forest? You see the forest here before you, but you cannot see the seeds that make it possible."

"Each forest is different. Is each gathering different, even though the medicine society is the same?"

"You know how old I am. This is the only Midewiwin I shall see, so you must ask your grandfather. My sense is that just as with woodlands, each will be different because the land and the wind and the water and the people are different."

Peewit sighed: "There is just so much to see."

The Shaman's Child

A hush had fallen and Peewit stood. The final group of the society was ready to enter the lodge, there were only seven. His aunt and grandfather came last with the blind healer, Loneseer, led by a small girl. Loneseer was often mentioned when his mother and grandfather spoke of difficult healing. He used his hands as others used plants and words, and Peewit had heard many tales of the ways his hands could see the bones of the body. Now Peewit looked to him first. The shaggy headdress was above the opaque eyes, and he shuffled carefully when he moved. Yes, he was different from the others, for Peewit understood that he did not need to see because he knew where he was and where he was going. The little girl stumbled and Loneseer said something to her with a smile. She looked to him with great pride.

Another voice interrupted and Peewit saw that his aunt was talking to the girl. How very brilliantly the patterns on her robe shone. Even the buffalo horns seemed to glitter. The medicine rattle she carried seemed huge, and she had painted one side of her face black and the other white. She alone of the seven wore an eye mask, and Peewit mourned for the goldfinch and orioles whose feathers he recognized.

"What is she called?" asked the Arapaho woman.

"Dancing Light."

"How does she make the colors so bright and everything shine like water?"

"I think she must mix flakes of the shining stones, mica, which crumble easily, into her dyes, and with the fat she rubs on the horns," Peewit said his thought aloud.

Chapter III

"Have you done that for her?"

"No, but I have found the shining mica often for those who make a powder."

"Hush" scolded a neighbor.

Peewit recognized in the stillness that his grandfather was watching. His feet, which Peewit had rubbed with sage, kept the steady pace of the drum, step, pause, step, even though the procession was not moving at all. He wore bells at his ankles and on the beaded bands beneath his knees. Peewit knew how they could shiver, just like a medicine rattle, but they were silent now. His leggings were decorated with quillwork and Peewit wondered why they drew his eye more than the rainbow worn by his Aunt, Dancing Light.

"Is it my love which sees him as so different?" Peewit wondered. He looked to his grandfather's face and saw the expression he called the hawk look. In this moment his grandfather would not even hear a question, let alone answer it. Why did his grandfather's white hair blowing slightly in the breeze seem so much more powerful than the horn headdresses worn by the others?

There was a ripple of sound, insistent, and the procession moved forward. Peewit was ashamed that even though he was watching he had not seen how his grandfather made the bells shiver. The old Arapaho was startled when the chant began; the high vibrato pierced all ordinary sounds. The seven voices lifted and carried, while the antiphonal singing from within the lodge came from all the apprentices. Then, at last, Loneseer and his little guide led the way into the lodge, the sacred time had begun.

The Shaman's Child

It took Peewit all of his discipline to wait beside the Arapaho as the others moved into the darkness ahead, but at last his father and others came to lift and carry the old medicine man into the lodge. Peewit's sister made a face at him as he passed, she had a place near the door and he knew she was teasing him for his long wait. He had made a promise, to stay with the man and now he moved in the shadow of the litter, unable to see where they were going. At last the dying man's willow back rest was in place, and Peewit could look around and see where they were.

Behind them and on either side, like a horse's hoof, the families were settling to watch and listen. Above them, the boughs of the roof of the lodge filtered the light, and only at the center was there a smoke hole through which the sun could shine directly. Before them, in rows by rank, sat the members of the medicine society. Many were setting out the contents of their medicine bundles. Others were lighting pipes. Loneseer and grandfather were talking, bending, and flexing their muscles. Peewit saw his mother looking over the crowd and knew she would have found each of her children and no matter what she performed during the ceremonies, she later would have a comment for any behavior which had caught her eye.

"Are you comfortable?" the Arapaho woman asked the old man.

"No, but I do not expect to be. Peewit, tell me what will happen."

The little boy was puzzled, for he had not seen this particular gathering before, so how could he say what it would bring? But then he replied:

"First come the greeting songs, then the separate prayers by each rank, and then by each leader will pray. Sometime near sunset, many

Chapter III

will play the hand games."

"Does the drumming change?"

"No, only for the games, and even then it is behind the other drums."

"Fix-it Find-it," called a cousin, "are you allowed to leave the lodge?"

"No," said Peewit quickly, hoping it was true.

"Pity, I have lost my pipe."

Before them, the band's leader moved to the center and began to beat his hand drum with the one-two sound of the deep drums. The long slow greeting songs began each verse and cadence announcing another aspect of the tribe's life. Long before the first song was finished, the old Arapaho was asleep. Peewit listened to the rattle of his breathing as if it too was part of the drumming.

Hour after hour the singing went on. Everyone sang, the very young without words, the very old without rhythm, and there was no distinction between good and bad singing, it was all a blessing of the gathering together. Peewit had been told by his sister that the songs were about spirits and if he listened he would hear how the others found their visions. Peewit heard songs to the winds and to the birds that knew how to fly with the winds. He heard greetings to everything that moved—water and animals, rocks upon the mountains, prairie fires and cooking fires. He did not hear anything referred to as a spirit. He watched his mother come forward to sing of plants. He would not let her voice put him to sleep.

Her songs were invocations to all growing things; she praised the strengths and held each on high so that all could see. Peewit heard no words about spirits and he knew his mother would leave nothing out of her song. New singers came but Peewit found it hard to listen and to think about what he was hearing. The Arapaho asked to be taken out so Peewit wiggled forward to ask permission of one of the guards. At the next pause he and the Arapaho were outside the lodge, the silent camp a strange contrast to the crowd within. Peewit wiped the old man's face as the spasm of sickness passed.

"I am sorry you are missing even part of the ceremony."

"I find it hard to listen and to think as I listen."

"Thinking must come later, my friend, just let all you see and hear fill you up like a cup."

"I don't know how to stop my questions."

"No, you may learn that later, but for now let the songs fill you with their own power."

"I want to see the hand games."

The Arapaho laughed.

"So did I at the beginning of my life, now at the end I know they are not for me."

"Are you in much pain today?"

"Now and then. Tell me, Peewit, what is your grandfather's name?"

Chapter III

"He is Running Wind."

"You do not know my name, I am called Low Horn."

"Why do you wish to know grandfather's name?"

"I take it with me; it makes the journey ahead less lonely if I know it."

"I do not understand about names."

"That is what this gathering is about, making names and sharing names."

"Come back," said the strong man who carried the Arapaho, "the leader will sing and we must not disturb him." They returned to the tent and Peewit was for the first time shy as he felt the eyes watch as they reentered the sacred ground.

This time as he listened, Peewit heard the songs differently. As the plants and animals and birds were named and their representatives sang a greeting, Peewit heard the attention of the crowd and the excitement of the singers.

"They are making it all new again, here," he whispered with awe to the Arapaho.

"Yes," smiled the old man, "and you are part of it."

The Shaman's Child

Chapter IV

Chapter IV

Peewit was surprised when his father stood to sing. It was easy to forget that he was a member of the medicine society because he did not visit the sick, or seek healing plants. The Arapaho woman was snoring loudly, so Low Horn wakened her just as Peewit's father began.

Peewit strained to hear what his father would name. The sounds came, tumbling, one upon the other, the cadence steady, but a puzzle. The meaning was hidden. Peewit closed his eyes. He heard the rustling restlessness of his neighbors, someone's stomach protested the long fast, and someone else was scratching, Low Horn's lungs rattled. And then it was as if Peewit was in the forest and he had closed his eyes to better hear a bird's song.

His father was greeting words: he was singing to the languages that all men shared and to their songs. Peewit stared across the gathering. His father sang with his head back and his eyes closed, the drum behind him was steady. Now Peewit heard that this was a greeting song to the gift of talk. In it, he understood why his father was a member of the medicine society, for he was singing the good words that might bring peace and understanding. He sang a greeting to the healing of songs, and even to the power of casual talk. Peewit felt eyes on him and glanced at once toward his grandfather. Had he smiled? Peewit closed his eyes again and listened to his father.

At last the greeting was done and it was time to form the teams for the hand games. Peewit was summoned by his mother to fetch water for the singers. Loneseer's guide did not want Peewit to hold the cup, but the blind man reached out to gently draw Peewit to him.

"You are Running Wind's grandson? You are the boy who they say does not see visions?" Peewit could only nod. The searching hand was still upon his face so Loneseer understood.

"Do not be ashamed, Child, what you see is your own, what others call it does not matter. I am blind, but I see in my own way. Thank you for the water."

"I see visions every day," said the small guide as Peewit passed by; he wrinkled his nose at her as if she was his sister.

"Fix-it, Find-it, I am very thirsty." Dancing Light had taken off her mask, and Peewit watched her drink. She was even more puzzling without the mask.

"You examine me carefully? Do you expect to find something in my face? It is too old to fix, I think," and she laughed a harsh and glittering laugh.

"I was wondering why you alone wear an eye mask for the greeting songs," Peewit asked cautiously.

"The better to protect you from all the dangers of my eyes," she

Chapter IV

replied but she was not really laughing now. Peewit moved on with the water.

"If you frighten our helper, Dancing Light, we shall all go thirsty," one of the younger men spoke from under his buffalo horns. First the leader of the gathering drank, and nodded his thanks to Peewit. Then the boy turned to his grandfather.

"And did she frighten you?" he asked, and Peewit heard the laughter behind the question.

"I think she says silly things because of her own fears."

"Do not call another silly Peewit, because you do not walk their path."

"I am sorry, but I do not understand why the Aunt does not wish others well."

"Watch the hand games. How is our Arapaho friend?"

"His breath hurts him now. His name is Low Horn."

"Have you told Low Horn, who gave you the gift of his name, that you will blow his whistle upon the death platform?"

"No," whispered Peewit.

"I think he waits to hear what you will do."

The drums began again. Peewit returned to his seat and saw that Low Horn looked very weak.

The Shaman's Child

"You have waited, now the hand games begin."

"My grandfather says you also wait," Peewit whispered, and then strongly he added "I promise you, Low Horn, I shall blow the bone whistle at the platform."

"Thank you, Child, and thank Running Wind for me. Now enjoy the games."

Low Horn's eyes closed and there were now long, long pauses between his breaths. It was sometime before Peewit turned away to look at the teams. The young initiates were too excited, handling the bone sticks of the holy game awkwardly. The drumming quickened, the songs were fast, and the leader dropped his hand. On each team the first player began. The bone sticks were small enough for a hand to conceal them, but between each team stood ten upright sticks. The holder of the bones tried every form of movement to conceal which hand held the marked bone while the others sang. Each time a guess was wrong, the team holding the bones claimed one of the ten sticks, but when the guess was right, a stick and the bones passed to the opposing side. The daily game was played to gamble, but here, it was the skills and the speed which were competing. The lodge was noisy with drums and the clapping of the sticks.

Peewit moved from team to team, watching the hands and the faces. He saw that those who did not play tried to mimic the gestures of those who were playing. He saw that sometimes a player's mouth worked with anxiety, and when he watched the eyes he became confused. He found himself opposite Dancing Light, who was playing against the experts, though it was not yet her turn.

She was intent, watching the guessers. Peewit thought as he looked

Chapter IV

at her that it was like watching a hovering owl; he dared not take his eyes from her but he needed to sense when the prey gave her a signal. His mother moved behind him, always singing slightly off key, and slightly slower than all the others. But there it was, the moment when the owl's eyes blinked, but this owl did not dive, instead she smiled and moved her gaze to the next team member.

Now Peewit did not watch the Aunt, but watched what she watched. This time he knew what he saw, for the moment came when the guesser reached his limit and tightened a muscle in resolution. Now he would guess, no matter what the holder of the bone was doing. The Aunt was indeed the owl; she was waiting for each moment of fear by which the guessers betrayed themselves.

When it was her turn to hold the bones, her hands were dazzling: first the wings of a frightened bird, then a dragonfly, then rain upon water. Everywhere she could reach, the Aunt sent her hands, faster and faster, and the guessers betrayed themselves, and she won, keeping the bones. The last stake stood, watchers crowded, and the final player shivered. When she challenged him and he had guessed, she did not open her hands but suddenly looked at Peewit.

"Fix-it Find-it, is he right, do I hold the bone in my left hand?"

"No, Dancing Light, you do not," answered Peewit quickly.

"You are right, and so I win," she said, but her smile was not of victory as she watched Peewit move away. He wondered why his breath was hard.

One of his cousins asked him "Have you seen Loneseer play?"

The Shaman's Child

"No."

"Go, before he tires, it is a wonder, a true vision."

"They treat me like one of the guessers of the games, as if having a vision is keeping something hidden," thought Peewit as he moved into the crowd watching Loneseer play.

After a moment Peewit almost laughed aloud, for Loneseer was doing exactly what mother birds did to distract an enemy from her hidden chick. The blind man's movements were slower than those of Dancing Light, and they were concentrated right in front where everyone could see. Peewit felt strange and then realized Loneseer's movements were timed by the drum, and although the beat was fast, the hands seemed much slower than the Aunt's hands. Peewit looked at the hands, just as if he was watching the mother bird in the forest. Loneseer did not move the bones at all, just as the hidden chick did not move. They remained in one hand, even as both hands moved as the mother bird's wings.

Time and again the opposing team took the movement for a transfer, so soon Loneseer had also won. Peewit listened to the teams discuss the movements and was astonished to hear complicated explanations. At last, it was almost dark, and the shadows made the grunts and guessing even more tense.

Peewit watched his grandfather play against the young initiates to the society. In his grandfather's hands the bones were in full view, not hidden at all. The drum was frenzied, the words of the game were shouted, but the bones rolled slowly, calmly, over and around grandfather's fingers. Peewit was startled when the fists closed and the challenged player was asked where the bones were. The song

Chapter IV

began again. This time Peewit watched the guessing team to see if Running Wind was watching for the signs of betrayal, but no, grandfather was not watching. Again he challenged, again he won.

The little boy thought to himself that he was not watching as he would in the forest, as he had with Loneseer. He was letting his feelings for grandfather change the way he watched. Now when the drum began, Peewit thought of grandfather as a great tree and the hands were nuthatches playing on the bark.

Now, Peewit understood. The hands never changed pace, they were all slow movements with Running Wind's breath, and there was no trick at all except that everyone was expecting a trick so did not see what was happening. When the game was over and Running Wind gathered his sticks, Dancing Light's voice sliced across Peewit.

"Did you dare, Running Wind, to ask Fix-it Find-it if your challenger was right? He knew mine was wrong, and I saw him smile as he watched Loneseer. Did you test him?"

There was mockery of the game, of the grandfather and of their affection in her voice, and when Peewit looked at his Aunt's face he was shocked to see the pain and the loneliness written on it.

"It would not be fitting," said Peewit, "for I am not even an apprentice, and this is still a sacred time."

"That did not stop you from answering me."

"Your game was ended and the drums were still. The drums still beat for the Leader."

The Shaman's Child

"They will half the night if he does not improve. Show us all Running Wind…"

But her challenge was cut off by a cry from the Arapaho woman. Peewit was running even before he heard Low Horn call for him. Quickly the sick man was carried back to the camp, but the elders would not let Peewit stay, and ordered him back to the lodge for the first of the long sweats.

Peewit met his mother and sisters, behind them Dancing Light. He told his mother what had happened but she did not speak. The little guide of Loneseer broke away from the procession and spoke to him.

"Since I must join the women for the sweat, my uncle asks that you join him. Hurry please Fix-it Find-it."

Peewit glanced up at the Aunt as they passed, once again she wore a mask, but now the boy could see the pleading which was almost like hunger on the face. Why had he not seen it before?

"Because I was just like the others, I saw what I expected to see," he thought and stumbled against Loneseer at the edge of the lodge.

"Good my young friend, you have found me. Can you find a place where my back will be against a pole? My bones are too old to hold me straight through the long night of sweats."

Peewit did not know when in the darkness his grandfather took him upon his familiar lap. He could feel Running Wind's breathing slow, and his muscles ease, and even with the singing and the laughter around them, nothing mattered except grandfather. Peewit wakened to feel his grandfather laughing.

Chapter IV

"Loneseer asked if you asked questions in your sleep, and I told him yes, always."

"Why do the old sleep less than the young?" asked Peewit as he rubbed his eyes.

"Now it is my turn to question, what have you seen this day?"

"Grandfather, do you mean everything?" Again, the two old men laughed.

"Everything, from the beginning," Peewit could hear that he was being teased.

"I saw that the greeting, even with the procession, makes things new again. It is not that the things themselves are changed, but by making a special day and a special song to name them once more we are changed. Like seeing new green shoots through the snow, and you recognize them but are surprised."

"Is that a vision?"

"No, no, it is doing something which makes a different way of seeing, not a seeing which makes the doing different."

"And what did you see in the hand games?"

"I saw that if there are five watchers of one player, they will see five different things. I saw that we fool ourselves, the player does not fool us, for we only see what we expect to see."

"Tell me more, Peewit."

"Dancing Light challenges her partner the moment she sees that he has chosen an expectation and he has settled on one view. Loneseer plays as the mother bird, knowing that the stalking hunter watches movement not stillness. You know that the watchers expect to be fooled by a trick, so you give them no trick, just ordinary movement, and they are fooled."

"So, now everything is clear and we may sleep without more questions?"

"No."

"At least some things are not even changed by our ceremonies," said Loneseer and Running Wind laughed as he held Peewit against him.

"Ask?"

"Why is Dancing Light so lonely, and is she sick that she is in pain?"

"He does have visions, that little one," commented Loneseer quietly.

"I think I should let you seek the answer yourself. Perhaps when you see us all compete on the final day you will learn more."

Peewit was quiet and in a moment Loneseer spoke again.

"His stillness is more demanding than our drumming. Speak, Boy, what is your next question?"

"Why do some of the singers and players let fear change the ways they sing or play, so that even though they have more skills than another, they seem to have less?"

Chapter IV

"Explain."

"In the long procession, the new initiates who are most frightened lose their places even as they determine to do well. In the songs, those who try to just sing the words and make the songs sing better than those who wait for murmurs from the crowd or fear that they hear none."

"What happens to the bird which shows its fear?"

"It is caught."

"Why?"

"That is my question, grandfather, not yours."

Both old men laughed. Peewit's father came to join them and asked:

"So, my son, did you find laughter in our singing?"

"No, Father, But I learned as I listened to you why it is that words alone also heal. You are also a healer and I did not know that before."

"Neither did I," said his father.

"Do all words heal?"

"No, Grandfather, just as the plants named by my mother can be used as poisons or to help heal, if words are not meant to help, they may harm."

"Hush Child, does my son try to teach my father?" Peewit's father sounded hurt in the darkness, and frightened.

Loneseer replied: "Your son is part of this sacred time and we are being made young by him. Did you not hear his pride as he spoke of you?"

"Yes, I am sorry I scolded."

"Father, is there word of Low Horn?"

"Yes, he lives still, but no longer knows who is beside him."

"What will happen if he dies during the sacred time?"

"You will have to go out with the young men and take his body high where the wind can dry it."

"You will not be there?"

"No, we of the society must stay, but you can do it without me."

"I said I would blow the bone whistle. He said I must thank you."

"Then you must be our substitute."

Peewit felt Loneseer's hand upon his face, and soon he slept.

His father spoke quietly.

"Is he not too young to go and make a platform for the dead?"

"He was not too young to be given a bone whistle."

Chapter IV

"He has seen many deaths already."

"Has he? I know so little." His father stood and moved away.

After the songs to the dawn were over and the preparations for the long initiations were underway, word came that Low Horn was dead. Peewit went out with his father and waited while three men who were not members of the medicine society were chosen to carry the body. His grandfather was occupied with the ceremony, so the only words of guidance to Peewit were his father's command "Be sure to sweat before you return to the lodge."

Low Horn's wife was tying up his medicine bundle when they came to her. Peewit knelt beside the corpse and touched it gently.

"He is not there, Child, he waits on the wind for you to blow his whistle."

Peewit helped her to bind the old man's body in a robe and the young men then bound him to carrying poles. They were a small procession, a shadow of the gay group of women they passed on their way out of camp.

"Fix-it, Find-it, go ahead and clear a trail."

"Where do we go?"

"To the north ridge and the place with the scars of an old fire."

It was not a long journey, three miles at most, but it took them tedious struggles to get over the deadfalls and brush at the edge of the forest until they were high on the ridge. Peewit climbed and bound the poles in a dead tree, and the men hoisted the body high up on to his platform in the wind. Peewit watched the breeze catch his long white hair and blow it, screening the dead face. He wondered if here there was ever a moment without wind, and he looked west. Yes, the mountains were there, a strange uneven horizon inviting Peewit, as they always did, to come and explore.

"Our job is done, now it is your turn. Buffalo Bird will stay with you and Low Horn's woman; we go down to build a sweat house at the base of the hill. We will wait for you there."

Low Horn's wife stood facing the wind, her eyes closed. She was singing, without sound.

Peewit took off his shirt and sat facing the body, into the wind. He pulled out the bone whistle and held it, not sure what to do. There should be words, he knew, a song for Low Horn's spirit to ride. Perhaps it was enough that his wife was saying prayers in the Arapaho language. No, if that was so, he would not have been asked to come and blow the whistle. Peewit felt very small, and looked behind him. Buffalo Bird was waiting, the old woman's lips no longer moved, she slumped forward, turned toward Peewit. He looked up at Low Horn and remembered the sigh of relief when he had agreed to blow the whistle. At last he put it to his lips and blew, unsure, afraid, and very lonely.

The sound which came from the whistle was caught by the wind, at once magnified.

"Ah," said Buffalo Bird, "the sound of the soul at death and now he shall be released." He nodded to the boy and lit his pipe.

Chapter IV

Peewit blew again, thinking now of the woman behind him and her long walk away from her own people so that Low Horn could see the medicine gathering before his death. He thought of the pain of the travois for the sick man, of the crossing of the hills and the prairie, and of their first dusty meeting when he carried spring water.

He thought of Low Horn and his father trying to become friends because they shared a language and of evenings by the fire when his grandfather and Low Horn shared their memories. He thought of his mother and the Arapaho woman, now weeping behind him, massaging the old body to ease his pain, and smiling to each other as they shared the tasks of giving care. He thought of the great festival, of the processions, the naming, and the games and of the sweats and dances yet to come.

As he thought he blew his thoughts into the flute, and gave sound to the last days of Low Horn's life and the love the old man had given him. The wind grew stronger as the morning lengthened and suddenly blew the robe from over the body, so that he was no longer separated from the sky and the earth. Peewit was very tired, and the bone whistle fell against his chest. Low Horn's wife touched his shoulder.

"Come, Child, you have released him, he is free. We must go down now."

Buffalo Bird led and Peewit often stumbled as though unfamiliar with his own body as he followed the familiar path. When they reached the little sweat lodge, Peewit slept a little while Buffalo Bird told the others of his piping. The walk back was silent; the Arapaho woman came slowly at a distance until she left them to go to her tent alone. Peewit followed the men into the sacred lodge.

The Shaman's Child

The initiations were over and the new members were sweating after their dance of celebration. The drum's beat was as steady as ever, and Peewit realized now it was the time of the medicine bundles. Each owner sat behind the bundle, some were open, some closed, and the crowd shuffled and chanted around the treasures. Peewit joined the line and found himself looking at two of his sisters who were with his mother.

"I am sorry, I did not hear you," he said.

"I asked if you were quiet because you are under the spell of a stranger's ghost."

"And I asked if you saw a vision at last when you blew the whistle?"

"You are not to talk, remember?" Peewit's father's voice surprised him, but his sister's looked frightened. His father guided the little boy away from the crowd and together they sat in a dark corner for a time.

"Buffalo Bird said you did well. If you are hungry you should eat, there will be fasting tonight."

"No, but I am thirsty."

To his surprise, Peewit's father handed him a cup of water.

"Will Low Horn's wife try to return to her people?" he asked.

"She will travel with us when we move south." Peewit could not see his father's face but he could feel a great restlessness long before he heard the question.

Chapter IV

"Tell me, why when your sisters or brothers laugh, you frown or seem puzzled, but as last night, when Running Wind and Loneseer laugh, there is laughter all around in the air and you laugh with them?"

"My sisters and brothers, and some grown-ups like Dancing Light, seem to laugh with pain or fear, and I do not understand that laughing. But Loneseer and my grandfather laugh when all things are right, and that laughter is inside me too."

"Do you sometimes feel it when you are alone?"

"Yes, often, and I think the wind and earth and all things feel it."

"Last night I wanted to laugh, but there had been no joke."

"But this is different from the laughter that follows a joke or a story."

"Is it magic?"

"I do not know what magic is, Father. If you mean is it like the hand games, no it is not that. It is more real."

"This ceremony causes strange things; I even ask questions of my son."

"I like what the ceremony is doing."

"That is good to hear," said Loneseer, sitting beside the boy.

"Do you need anything, Loneseer?" asked Peewit's father.

"No, but I thank you. Is the child eating that he asks no questions?"

The Shaman's Child

"He has fallen asleep. Perhaps he should not have gone to play the flute. He seems very small still."

"He went and it is over. He was big enough to make a promise and keep it. You sound uneasy?"

"Yes, I have been telling others they may not talk and have been asking questions of my smallest son."

"The sacred time changes each of us. Let it do its work. Outside the lodge we need strong rules, but here become a stranger to the rules."

"Making new again," said Peewit, awakened by the talk between his father and Loneseer.

"What did you say?"

"The sacred time is making us new again, Low Horn felt it too."

"But if that is so why did he not feel he could be cured by it?"

"There is no cure for dying, even in the sacred lodge. It would be wrong to ask for that."

"The truth of things is to die, and Low Horn accepted that. I think we can ask anything if we ask it of ourselves only. What would be wrong," said Loneseer "would be to ask another to break the patterns of all things."

"You mean if Low Horn, even as he knew he was dying, had expected my mother or Running Wind to cure him, and had come to the gathering only for that, that would be wrong?"

Chapter IV

"Yes, as I see it."

"But he did not come that way."

"On the journey he did not say why he came, only that he wished to see it before he died," said Peewit's father.

"He came for the making new and the sharing of names," said Peewit.

"What do you mean the sharing of names?"

"He called the many greeting songs that, he said when we sang and made the lists of all that we know, we were sharing names and making all things that we know new again to the listeners. Each hears it or says it in his own way so that when a stranger comes or a new apprentice is accepted, that way becomes a part of all that we know, and is also new again."

"I do not think I understand."

"But Father, you said the same thing when you sang your greeting song to the words, and you sang of bringing peace and joining strangers through words."

"Yes, I sang that." There was silence for a long time, and then Peewit's father walked away. Peewit sighed.

Loneseer teased him "Have you too much breath?"

"It would please my father if I did not ask questions, and if I would see visions."

"Do you truly think if you did see visions you would not ask questions?"

"That would depend on the vision," said Peewit, and suddenly the two were laughing and all those who heard them smiled.

The medicine bundles were blessed and tied away, the drummers for the great dance gathered in the center of the lodge. One of Peewit's cousins pinched him and ran away and soon Peewit was dancing, dusty and relieved by the activity. During the night it rained so in the dawn prayers all who gathered raised their arms into the mist and were glad this was the last great day. Peewit listened to the talk around him.

"I say Loneseer will win again, no one can remember when he did not win." One of Peewit's sisters was arguing with Loneseer's little guide.

"This time I think Dancing Light will win."

"She cannot heal bones as he can."

"But he does not drive away danger from a place as she does."

"Maybe she brings it with her so that she can drive it away."

"No one ever sees the bones that Loneseer heals."

"If you can walk or use your bow again, you do not need to see the bone."

The arguments drifted across the camp, some cousins even gambling about who would be champion. When the competitions began,

Chapter IV

first ranks were quickly decided. Some of the initiates could not even imitate an owl accurately, thought Peewit. He was seated to the south-east of the central pole, for he wanted to watch carefully without looking into any sunlight.

For a time it seemed that every performer ended with a hoop dance or some other display of great agility, so Peewit found he was restless while those around him cheered. The lodge was warm, and he noticed already the leaves on the branches were dry. How quickly this summer was passing. They would have to move south as soon as the festival ended. The crowd was suddenly quiet.

Loneseer was being led to the center pole. He was dressed in beaded leggings and wore the buffalo horn headdress. The companion girl strutted, Peewit thought, as if she was going to dance. When Loneseer dropped her arm and stood to pray, she did not sit, but watched the crowd. Peewit listened to the words.

How did Loneseer make the sound of the stream when he spoke of water and the warnings of the wind when he called upon the power of air? Peewit listened with his eyes closed and heard the soft reinforcement of the drum behind the voice and realized that Loneseer spoke with the timing and the color in his voice of whatever he was describing. Peewit heard the ending of the prayer coming before the others, so his eyes were open and he was tense when Loneseer summoned all the powers of healing he had used in his long life to be with him now, in this moment.

A boy beside Peewit said "This should be good, he always wins." But Peewit was intent, something else was coming.

"My friends," said Loneseer, "you have paid me the honor of having me stand first in this society. I wish to remind you that the honor is not to me, but to the power that is in us all as we live and walk the land. Today I do no more displays for you." Cries of disappointment sounded like a chorus.

"No, for we have gathered to teach and to share what we know with each other and to be sure that what we do when we are called to heal will bring peace, and will heal. I cannot let you think that my hands are as fast or as smooth as once they were, for you might ask me to help someone in pain and I must tell you that my hands are failing me."

Peewit grunted. A boy beside him poked him to be quiet.

"The pain we see in the joints which swell is no longer mine to remove, but now mine to bear, so I cannot use my hands again since they may, against my wishes, cause harm." Loneseer paused and removed the buffalo headdress and put it gently on the earth at his feet. Peewit felt the attention draw together like a thrown spear.

"Yet, though I do not use my hands, I am still a healer, so in farewell, I shall sing the Manitou's dream."

Years later in the sweat house, men would turn to Peewit and ask him "Tell of the time the great Loneseer sang the Manitou's dream" for by then they knew that Peewit was the only one who remembered. And in all of the times when Peewit told the story, he began: "It was at the height of the morning on the third day of the gathering and we were very warm in the lodge."

But this day, Peewit brushed the sweat from his eyes and watched Loneseer circle on one foot, establishing the pace of the song. The

Chapter IV

drum never varied. The crowd waited. Peewit expected the song to begin as all prayers did, with a wail, a high call for attention. But when he saw the muscles of Loneseer's belly contract and waited for the coming sound it was not as he expected. For a moment he thought there was no sound, but then he heard it, deep, like the bittern's call, as slow as almost to be the great drum itself. The boy beside Peewit squirmed, nearly frightened. Peewit listened and understood, Loneseer was singing the pulse, even his own, just as grandfather would match his breathing to Peewit's during sleep.

Loneseer was singing of sleep, of the Manitou's restlessness in the darkness, of the sudden sense of falling and waking before he breathed again with the pulse of his blood. Though it was bright morning in the lodge, many dosed and felt the night of the Manitou cover them. Now Loneseer's voice changed, and as it did, Peewit heard the impatience of growing things and the lapping water. Loneseer was using words not to tell of things he had done but to bring things out of the memory of each listener.

Peewit heard the old voice sing of life in the waters and thought of the first curled ferns, and he heard the excitement of frogs greeting the warm air from the mud. How did Loneseer do it? Before him there stood only an old blind man, bathed in the soft light, the shadows of the drummers barely visible behind him. But the voice filled all of Peewit as it filled the entire lodge, and yet it was not loud. Now it sang of the birds above the waters and their songs of delight as they chose their mates and built their nests. Each of the names of the greeting songs came again to Peewit's memory and the Manitou's world filled with a sense of urgency.

Suddenly, Peewit thought of the many times when others laughed at him, and in that bright morning he shivered. Loneseer sang of the Manitou's loneliness that in all the busy world of his dreams there was none who recognized him. The boy beside him was cold, and clutched at Peewit's arm: "Is this death, does he sing of dying?"

"No, he sings of no one to greet anything, ever," and Peewit watched as Loneseer's arms began to rise and the pace of the drum began to race. The voice was shrill, and Peewit felt tears and a need for his grandfather so great that he almost moved. But no, he must watch; even if he let his tears fall. The drum stopped. Loneseer's hands were open, empty, reaching into the emptiness above him. Was no one in the lodge breathing? The old man's fingers began to quiver like feathers in the wind. Then there was a rustle of grass and leaves, the ankle bells Peewit thought, startled. Now, Loneseer's voice came differently and the words were laughter and relief and surprise and his hands danced with the drum. The Manitou was making a friend, a singer who was not an echo. When the friend walked upon the grass and bathed in the waters, the two danced and the Manitou's breath was excited. Slowly it eased, slowed, and once again was the deep, deep pulse. The Manitou slept at peace, the dream was done.

In the great clamor that followed, the girl did not return to guide Loneseer. The crowd was busy stretching and settling, and Peewit saw that Loneseer did not move.

"She has gone out, I believe, do you need help to find a place?" Peewit asked the old man.

"So, it is you, no wonder they call you Fix-it Find-it. I do not wish to be close to the drums, I am spent."

"Come, there is space near the walls of the lodge."

Chapter IV

"But you must not stay, go and learn until the sacred time is over, then we will meet again."

Peewit again watched from where he did not look into the sunlight. He puzzled over the song after others had competed, they were clumsy, he thought. Then a man and a woman competed together, sometimes mocking, then too solemn, and Peewit thought of magpies. Now Dancing Light stood in the center of the lodge.

There was not a single color which she had not used, but Peewit did not think of the rainbow as he watched her. She was festooned with rattles and claws but her sleeves were so heavy they betrayed the tricks before she had performed. The drum began, double time, and Peewit was dazzled. Her voice was a scream as she whirled in the sunlight. When at last she stood still, she produced a wand in each hand.

"Oh, the horsehair ferns," grinned Peewit as he recalled how often he had pulled and pushed the links of the fern together. Dancing Light's song was of the guardian spirits. She made them seem angry and distant. As she sang she did her conjuring and she was faster and cleverer than any before. Yet, Peewit could see that something was wrong, for he could see each ruse coming before she performed it, and to his growing puzzlement, she repeated each one twice, almost angrily. It was a long performance and Peewit turned to watch the crowd, maybe they could teach him what was happening. Most seemed casual, commenting on her skills to a neighbor, watching just a little, then turning away. Peewit watched the crowd, then Dancing Light, then the crowd again, and at last he understood.

There was no feeling from the crowd to Dancing Light, and no matter how hard she tried by the many clever feints and her piercing song, she could not change that. So this was why she was so angry, so frightened, and so lonely. This was the terror of the echo. The more he watched the more sorrowful Peewit became. Then for a moment Dancing Light's hands were still, but from them came a cloud of shadows and then within the shadows a glittering, catching the sunlight and bringing a final burst of applause from the crowd.

"Did you see? She brought the spirits to her and showed the lights of power within them?" The boy sounded frightened as he spoke.

"The lining of the wood duck's nest and the powder of the stones which shine," Peewit muttered. He was sorry for Dancing Light as he watched her remove her rattles. She kept looking for something in the crowd, but even as she sat panting, no one came near. Now and then she stared at the gathering of students talking with Loneseer.

To the side of the gathering Peewit saw his grandfather standing. It was his turn now. The crowd was eager, noisy; the sacred time was almost over. Grandfather moved in the shadows, first to one side, where he waited, then to another. "He is measuring something, what is it?" thought Peewit.

The leader of the assembly signaled and the drums began again slowly. Running Wind moved so that the sunlight struck only his chest, his face and his legs were in darkness. His chest was bare, and so were his arms, but in one hand he held a bark cup, and in the other the eagle's feather from his medicine bundle. He held his hands still, and the crowd grew silent. Peewit noticed that the cup and the feather looked different as they formed shadows on Running Wind's chest. He swallowed, nervously.

"Are you frightened for him, Fix-it? It is still a competition." His

Chapter IV

sister's voice startled Peewit, but he did not turn.

It was the same pulse, the same drumming that began Loneseer's song. But it could not be it was not permitted to repeat what had gone before. Peewit closed his eyes. No, it was similar, but the pulse was not the same. This was not the Manitou sleeping, yet here was grandfather's voice, low and summoning.

Peewit listened and watched and felt a great restlessness, almost like hunger, overcome him. The cup was now a canoe, and the feather became waves upon water. Had they themselves changed or was it only the shadows on Running Wind's chest which had changed? His hunger grew, but the waves grew still, and the feather was now a growing thing, pushing up at the edge of the waters. What was the song? It held no words, it was a humming against the drumming, a sense that this he must share; there was no choice except to share it.

"What spell does he cast that all now sing and sway without words?" a boy beside Peewit asked? But Peewit had closed his eyes to hear what he was seeing. Yes, it was like hunger, but it was in every part of him, not just his belly. If I touch the earth, it will be there too, he thought, and his eyes flew open with the idea.

The shadows, the cup and the feather had now turned to fish in the sea, or were they birds above it? Out of the humming came the birdsongs, the chortling of the waders and the lilt of the meadow-lark, yet somehow they did not remove the hunger. The sunlight shone almost directly from the smoke hole now, Peewit could see that Running Wind had moved so that only his hands and chest stayed in the light. How was the cup turned into a crawling thing, and how did grandfather make the soft chewing sound of a little furred animal? Peewit concentrated and saw that the slightest change of his grandfather's hands changed both the shadows on his chest, and the ways the cup and feather were linked to each other. He heard more chewing sounds and recognized the leg rattles were moving. How the hunger of the humming hurt, and how he wanted to know what it all meant!

Slowly, the sounds changed. Now there was an excitement: was something caught in a trap, was someone coming, perhaps he would see the mountains clearly at last, even though he was still climbing a hill. Peewit no longer sat, but crouched, and caught himself humming with all the others. What was grandfather doing?

The cup and the feather were lying quietly now, but in the lodge the humming was nearly a cry. The cup became a head, a head that had been sleeping. As the head rose, the feather became arms, the shadow was waking to turn and look at the world. Birdsongs were there in greeting, and running water and wind, but now, what was this coming? The head, or was the cup, or just the shadow, was now moving, standing, it was a man! Peewit laughed. Everyone was laughing. Running Wind's chest was rippling as the man, the cup and the feather in his hands went dancing.

At last there were words to the song. The greeting song to the sun, and everyone sang it, but Peewit heard that hunger was still there, still part of the song. Now, only Grandfather sang, and sometimes the man danced, or bent, or drew a bow. Then he began to fall, but the song still praised the sun. The cup was the head against the earth, then it became the earth, and a woman in front of Peewit was weeping. The song of words to the sun was not sad; laughter was within it, even as her tears were part of it.

Peewit watched as once more the feather became a growing sprout

Chapter IV

up through the earth; birdsongs became part of the sun song, and the furred creatures joined while the man was dancing, singing, dying, and the hand holding the feather dropped from sight. Only the cup and its shadow remained the sun with the prayer song. Slowly, slowly, the sun set away from Grandfather's chest, and the song turned again to the hungry humming.

The noon sunlight shone down and Peewit watched as Grandfather's breathing became the pulse of the drums, and the humming now was with the drums. He tried to hold his breath but could not, for his breathing joined the drum, with everyone in the lodge. Suddenly, there was no one there. Grandfather had stepped back. Only the sun, directly down, held the center of the lodge at its axis. A moment passed, another, and now Peewit did hold his breath. Then the crowd went crazy and Peewit laughed until his tears came. The boy next to him hugged him and then was astonished that he held Peewit. "What was it? What was the song of magic?" he asked.

"He answered the Manitou's dream. He sang the song of all that lives."

Peewit moved to sit against old, blind Loneseer.

"You found something in his song?" whispered Loneseer, but Peewit felt his body trembling and could not answer. The frenzied crowd finally became still as the leader of the sacred time stepped forward.

"You have heard and watched. Now you must choose a new head of the medicine society. Who will succeed Loneseer?"

"Running Wind" from all directions of the lodge the voices cried out happily, rejoicing in their leader. Peewit watched as his grandfather stepped out of the shadows. He carried his headdress lightly and put it on his head in view of the crowd. There was no need to speak. The crowd was clapping, dancing, ready now to be released for the great feast. The leader's prayer was short, and the crowd in a great surge carried Running Wind with them as they went out into the world to dance.

Late in the afternoon when the shadows were inviting, it was time for the Chicken dance. Peewit had watched the grand celebration until he could wait no longer. He tied the brown costume of feathers to his arms and back, but the Arapaho woman came to his aid before he joined the procession. He waited and watched as the older boys lead, but he was eager for he knew his feathers would not fall.

The boy who had been beside him in the lodge was dressed entirely in scarlet; one of his brothers was almost as bright as Dancing Light had been. As they passed, Peewit thought which plant had created which color. It was best to remind him of what he knew, always. At last it was his turn to join the procession at its end and begin to close the dance circle. He heard but was not disturbed by the mocking cries and the laughter as he walked. Yes, he was the boy who did not see visions, and yes, he was all in brown, but that was just like the prairie chicken, so he was happy.

The Hoop Dancers finished and the boys formed their wide circle. Always, always, the drums remained. The biggest of the boys began the prancing, shaking performance, round and round, twisting and stamping, pausing now and then to show off his costume. One after another they turned, posing, and the crowd watched and chatted, judging their growth as well as the dance. Then came Peewit.

He did not prance; he danced just as the prairie chicken danced, with

Chapter IV

only his feet moving, his wings down, his tail feathers drumming. Sometimes he would scuttle across the circle; his head thrust back threatening, just as the cock would do. Another time he would sigh, and droop and convey to all that this was a ridiculous thing for a bird to do, which they had all seen the chicken do. His wings did not wave as did those of the older boys. They fluttered, and he preened them, and they fluttered again. When the drums slowed, and the older boys stopped their circling, Peewit was very dusty, a thirsty little bird, and he left the circle, bobbing, in search of water. It took a moment for him to realize that the crowd was cheering him, and hands were pulling him back to join the dancers' circle. The sweat was in his eyes and he could not see who was calling, but the leader said they might join the feast. And that was all that mattered.

When the stars were bright and the fires had died low, Running Wind stretched out on the earth and drew Peewit against him.

"How many stars are there?"

"As many as there are seeds blown by the wind in all the springs and summers that have ever been."

"Can you count them?"

"No."

"Do you want to count them?"

"It is enough to know that they are there to look upon."

"What did you see on this day?"

The Shaman's Child

"I saw you show us what is real."

"Was it magic?"

Peewit laughed, and Running Wind laughed with him.

"You Grandfather, what did you see this day?"

"I saw a boy become a prairie chicken, and I heard a boy laugh when he saw a cup and a feather dance together."

Peewit did not answer. The old man watched the stars for a long time and then he whispered:

"It was real, and it was a mystery."

From within his sleep, Peewit answered "Yes."

Chapter V

CHAPTER V

Over the next years as Peewit counted his summers to eight, and then ten, the band always seemed to be moving. Now that Running Wind was the head of the medicine society, there were always gatherings to attend, new festivals each summer, new initiates to be taught, and before all else, the daily work of healing. Sometimes Peewit travelled with his father to listen to discussions over hunting territories or to assist some new chief move his band without conflict to join with neighbors. He was still Fix-it Find-it and to most of the band remained the boy who did not see visions, but his father's friends now called him Peewit and some even told strangers the story of the bone whistle. The Arapaho band always welcomed him as an adopted son, and after one journey, his father told Running Wind that it was Peewit's presence that caused the tribe to change its view of strangers.

"They said that before they feared that every rider who was not of their band might be dangerous, but now they knew that even those strangers might be bringers of gifts."

Peewit's mother had new students of the healing herbs, so there were more errands to run and puzzles to solve. Each spring when some young man went off to find a guardian spirit, the teasing would revive. Peewit found comfort playing the old bone whistle. He would sit very still in the forest, watching. When he would blow the whistle, birds responded to his call, knowing he did not hunt them.

In the autumn of his tenth year, he travelled to the far north with Running Wind. Sometimes they met Chipewyan people and Peewit was able to understand much that was said. They sat late into the night listening to the stories of the cold land without trees. Peewit wondered just how large the earth could be, and how many summers it would take to explore it. He almost asked the question, but he hesitated.

That evening he heard the tribe's leaders sing their greeting to the walking that claimed their world. He understood that here they felt that each step into a new land claimed that land for the walker. His question might have been taken to be war not curiosity. Early in the morning a tired rider from their own tribe came to see Running Wind.

"Loneseer lies dying, and asks if you can bring the boy who plays the bone whistle to him."

"How far away is he?"

"It has taken me eight days and nights, but we knew you were here in the north."

"Then he must not be dying quickly."

"No, but he knows and says he wants to greet you while he can still say what he wants to say."

Chapter V

The grandfather asked "Have you word of where my band goes for the winter?"

The messenger said "They go again to the coal country, near the great buffalo fall."

"In two days we will move east," said Grandfather. "Peewit, you must take the seekers to the forest, and I will spend time with the leaders in a sweat lodge."

Peewit had thought the strangers disliked having a mere boy show them the healing plants, but he learned that they trusted he would never poison them. A woman had said once of him "His will is still good". He had gnawed on that thought for many miles, and he stopped trying to hurry the lesson.

Only five of them made the slow trek eastward, Running Wind had sent all the rest to help prepare for the winter in the coal lands. Peewit thought he would wake one morning and find himself partly white from the cold like the rabbits and the ptarmigan in their mottled transition to winter camouflage. Running Wind teased him that he would have to make a new dance costume.

Twice there was heavy snow at night, and it took them fifteen days before they heard they were nearing Loneseer's camp.

"Why do we dislike each other so much that we stay so far apart?" Peewit grumbled.

"Maybe we enjoy our reunions more than companionship," said Running Wind.

The Shaman's Child

Loneseer's band had built a wood lodge, and the warmth was a shock to Peewit. The blind man lay near the smoke hole. His hands were transparent as they fluttered up to greet the visitors.

"You have come, my old friend? And is the boy with you, the Fixer and Finder?"

"We are both here, cold and hungry and tired, but warmed by your welcome."

The formal greeting was lengthy, and the two men held each other's hands while they repeated the slow, dignified phases. Peewit was fascinated for he heard the acute and painful feelings between the two expressed in these ritual words of greeting. These words were often used by warring tribes to negotiate peace, and now they were said in the time of dying to bring peace to friends. Peewit thought this was a making new again, like the great medicine festival.

"Have you grown? Come, they will bring you food."

There was little talk that first night, for a blizzard raged, and the horses were mournful when he went out in the morning to feed them. Peewit had found many familiar faces recalled from his wanderings, here he was always called Fix-it Find-it. He was disgusted when two little boys followed him and asked him to show them his spells for finding things. Women asked after his mother and how she might use this or that plant. Peewit thought they were testing him. He passed young men playing hand games and one of them asked

"Do you still not see visions?"

"How can anyone not see visions?"

Chapter V

"This is the grandson of the chief of the medicine society, but he sees no visions."

"Don't you feel lost without a spirit guardian?"

The disdain of the boys, coupled with his own loneliness, prompted Peewit to sit suddenly to play the hand game. This challenge was so obvious that others laughed, but no one insisted that Peewit leave. After a short time they played in earnest and the hand drum behind them seemed as fast as Peewit's heart.

The first three boys assumed that quick and flash play would defeat Peewit, but one after another they were eliminated. The next two players were clumsy and watched their own hands so did not fool Peewit. He could feel anger and puzzlement around him, but he felt a ferocity he had not known before. At last there was only one young man remaining, and Peewit held all the other stakes. The man started slowly, watching Peewit who was ashen and sweating. The confidence of the opponent soared and the chanting crowd was almost screaming. The man held out his clenched fists and without hesitation Peewit leaned out to the left and turned it over. There lay the bones. Peewit heard their whispered comments.

"It is not fair, the magician casts spells for him to win."

"He casts his own spells."

"It was not a real win since he used magic."

"There was no magic."

The Shaman's Child

"You are just a boy; you cannot win against our best players without magic."

At last Peewit rose and walked through the hostile audience to Loneseer's side.

"Victory does not please you?" asked Running Wind, gently.

"I feel I need a sweat bath."

"What do you wish to wash away?" asked Loneseer. Peewit looked at the blind eyes with great longing and finally spoke.

"They said I used spells and magic to make the winning easy. I merely watched what they did, as I do when I track an animal or bird to find its own place. But my watching is not for games and winning, and I feel I am less than I was because I used it against opponents who believe it is a making of spells."

"You are hurting inside?"

"Yes, my watching feels heavy sometimes, and yet if I did not have it I would be lost. Is it easier to be blind, Loneseer?"

"The gift is not to do with your eyes. You would be a watcher with ears if you were blind, or with your hands. The heaviness is the weight of your gift, and the gift will grow, not wither, as you use it."

"How do you see with your hands?" Peewit asked.

Loneseer put his hands on the boy's face and said nothing for a time. Then, quietly, he said only to Peewit: "Can you feel through my hands

Chapter V

that I understand you, Peewit?"

"Yes, yes," said Peewit, and his heart filled with peace again.

"That is all it is," said Loneseer. "I feel your loneliness and your peace through my hands, and I try to give you back my attention."

"Does paying attention heal?" asked Peewit, shyly.

"Yes, Peewit, true watchers are healers," said Loneseer. He sighed, and somehow Peewit knew that this was the teaching he had come to learn from the old man.

"Are you ashamed, Peewit that they spoke of magic?" Running Wind reached out and held the boy against him and in doing so realized how quickly Peewit was growing.

Peewit replied "Whatever they call magic is just our world as it is. Like the patterns of plants around a lake, or the way the flocks know to gather and go south away from winter. It is there perhaps to teach us if we watch, but not for use, not for tricks or for fear."

"Then," teased Running Wind, "It was you who told us Dancing Light used the tricks from her loneliness and fear."

"I believe her tricks are not magic, they are her skills, just as my mother knows how to make the medicines that work." said Peewit. "In this world many things are mysterious. Some people call what they cannot understand magic. The mysteries of what we seek to know will not be changed by us, and we must not use our gifts just because we want to win a game, or gain cheers from an audience."

The Shaman's Child

"It was not many summers ago that you said you did not know what magic was, now you know?" Running Wind reflected.

"Yes," Peewit agreed,"I do know now."

Running Wind chuckled as he asked "Even frightened men who must tease those who win against them in a hand game?"

"I suppose so Grandfather, though I wish there were not so many of them," Peewit laughed "And even more I wish I did not have to stay within this argument." Hearing them, Loneseer laughed, and Peewit could laugh again as well.

That night he slept well, and the next morning Loneseer lay dead.

Peewit again played the bone whistle into the wind though his loss and the cold made his lips tremble. Back at the lodge he asked Running Wind the question which was haunting them all.

"I am sorry that Loneseer did not teach us the healing of bones. Is there another who can teach us?"

The young woman who came hissed at Peewit "Do you still see no visions?" He was startled to recognize the little guide from the great festival of years ago. She had grown tall and had a shadowed face like Dancing Light. She took them to Morning Cloud; a very old woman who was the only one left who still knew how to mend bones.

Running Wind observed that her hands were swollen and she could not practice the skill. He was able to persuade Morning Cloud to teach what she knew. In order to feel the lessons of bone and sinew as she talked, Peewit found that he had to close his eyes and see

Chapter V

through his hands.

Day after day they practiced. Night after night the wind and snow battered at the lodge. The storm finally passed. Running Wind rode out into the white world leaving Peewit to learn.

Morning Cloud taught Peewit about splints and as she talked Peewit found her tone soothing.

The angry girl came and watched and began to tease.

"If you can see bones with your hands, why can you not see visions? I think, you are afraid."

Morning Cloud gestured to Peewit to continue his lesson and said "A boy who plays a bone whistle at the platform of the dead is not afraid. Don't be foolish."

The girl was disdainful: "I know I have a guardian and he does not. The boys he beat at the games with his spells all have found their guardian."

"There are no magic spells." Peewit glowered.

"I was there and saw the spells that Loneseer and Running Wind cast with their voices," said the girl. "Dancing Light is a better magician."

"The society is one of healers not magicians."

"Some say otherwise."

Morning Cloud asked, "If you think those who heal use fear, why

The Shaman's Child

do we seek plants?"

The girl said slyly "Maybe it tries to show that the shaman has done something besides sing."

"Has anyone sung for you?" Peewit asked suddenly.

Her face twisted with some pain and she ran off.

Morning Cloud explained the girl was an orphan whose band had starved. She had been adopted to serve as Loneseer's eyes.

"Now that Loneseer is dead, what will she do? It is hard to be without a place. She is still afraid and we cannot wipe out the time of starvation from her memory. So she still starves."

Morning Cloud was sleeping when Running Wind returned.

He said to everyone, "We shall go south in the morning, and we must travel as fast as we can, for we will have storms behind us all the way."

It was not until they rested on the third night that Peewit could ask questions again.

"Why do so many people feel lost and lonely even as they live with others?"

"What do you mean?"

"Think of Dancing Light or the girl who was Loneseer's guide or even Loneseer who did not have an apprentice. Each has a place within the tribe and there is always work to do. Why do they live

Chapter V

in pain?"

"And?"

"And do we not have a medicine for this sickness?"

"You have been thinking and learning new ways of healing with your hands. What path have your thoughts travelled?"

"It seems to me that there are those in our band who are at ease…"

"What is at ease?"

"I mean like the geese in marshlands who return again and again to nest, they do not attack those who share the marsh, feeding each other and greeting strangers. They are a part of everything around them."

"They belong to the marsh?"

"Perhaps, but it is not claiming the marsh, it is just being part of what is and respectful of what is."

"And who do you find live as part of what is within our band?"

"Those like my mother, who respects what the plants can do. She is always asking for more learning and more knowledge. She is always taking on more apprentices, and she does not think the band should change just because of what she knows or what she does."

"She might think a son or a daughter might change."

The Shaman's Child

"But that is no different from the way a mother coyote will nip at the pups."

"Is there another who is at ease this way?"

"I think of my father and uncles. They go where there is need, they try to bring peace, and most of the time I do not think they are afraid."

"But sometimes are they afraid?"

"Yes, Grandfather, but I think those who tease and mock a lot are often afraid."

"And those who are afraid are also lost?"

"No, not in the way that Dancing Light or the orphan are both afraid. I am sometimes fearful but when I am afraid I do not think I will cease to be Peewit."

Running Wind lay quiet, listing and waiting.

"I think, Grandfather, that those who are lost do not want the world to be as it is, and they fear their thoughts. That is why they are so sure there must be spells and magicians. They do not know what power rests in what exists, and not in them."

"So, if someone believes in spells you think they fear they may cease to be and lose who they are?"

"Yes."

Chapter V

"And?"

"And I think our singing, and the healing by plants and with hands appears to those who are afraid as if we can do them harm. Because they fear they may be lost, they expect nothing to be right or safe. They do not trust what is real."

"Yes."

"Yes?"

"Yes, I think that is the sickness of the mind, and always has been. There are those who do not know what is real and are trapped by their own fears."

"And is there healing? Is there a way to bring someone out of that fear?"

"Perhaps for some that is what the seeking of the guardian spirit achieves."

"Grandfather, you do not mock me?"

"No, no, but I do think that for some the seeking of a guardian quiets their fears."

"But that does not help them to know what is real."

"Have I told you that sometimes questions give my stomach pains like bad meat?"

"But there is so much to learn."

The Shaman's Child

"Try now to dream your answers."

"That works too."

Peewit said that so calmly and rolled into a ball so comfortably, he did not notice that Running Wind was alert. The old man listened to the breathing of the horses and the night wind. To the stars he said a simple prayer:

"Keep him pure and safe, once I am gone."

The thaw held for a month as they traveled south but as soon as they reached the winter camp there was no respite. For many weeks there was bitter wind. Running Wind was ill, as was Peewit's mother, and many others. Peewit grew thin and strong as he labored through the winter. Twice Running Wind's cough so frightened him, that Peewit went out into the snow to find rabbits for broth. He watched carefully to be sure that each morsel was swallowed. When, finally, his mother began to move about and watch Peewit, she saw that Running Wind would roll over on his furs after coughing, and Peewit would knead the old back with his hands.

"So, Loneseer taught you his gift?"

"No, Morning Cloud showed me how to use my hands, and I have learned a little."

"It helps your grandfather."

"It would help more if I knew what Loneseer rubbed upon his hands before he worked."

Chapter V

"Your sister's cough is harsh, see if you can ease her as well."

Peewit was the first to smell spring on the wind, and roused his father in the dark one morning with the news that there were travelers from the south.

Later it seemed that from that meeting all things changed for the bands of the foothills. The men were never able to stay in camp to play and feast and people came from every direction seeking Running Wind for guidance. His mother sent her apprentices and plants far away and kept Peewit foraging high in the hills for her supplies. The first from the far south brought news of seekers for furs and a poisoned drink, and of all those who shared their camps falling ill with strange diseases. Over the winter of Peewit's twelfth year, refugees from the east told the same tales.

"What are you seeking?"

"Safety to hunt again."

"Why have you left your lands?"

"A new tribe has come and brings sickness and poison. We fled so that we will not want their drink."

"Can you not make a treaty to share the land?"

"There is no trust for sharing when they kill more than they need."

Over and over Peewit asked Running Wind if this was the same disease as the feeling of being lost, and was there no help that they could offer. He stopped asking when he saw that his questions caused his grandfather pain. Running Wind stopped speaking for a month after they learned of the death of Dancing Light.

"The traders for furs have built a large wooden camp on the banks of the Red River," began the stranger. "They sent scouts asking for furs and with one of the scouts was a bundle with shining stones in many colors. These were passed from band to band until they reached Dancing Light. When she saw them she laughed and said she must have more, so that she could cover herself and truly become Dancing Light. All that winter she sent trappers out, and in the spring it took three travois to carry her load of furs. She travelled fast without heed to any greetings along the way, and those who saw her said her eyes did not see outward. Finally she met one of the new traders and said she had come for the shining stones.

"His eyes were dark as the furs he wanted, they say, but he had none of the colored stones. He only had the poisoned water. He talked with Dancing Light through some translator who said the water would give her all the magic she wanted. So she drank the poisoned water and gave him her three travois of furs, and she told the stranger her name."

Peewit felt the audience shudder, but there was still more to the story.

"It took three days, just as she had given three travois of furs. Each morning she would scream in pain that she had no more magic, and each morning the trader would say she needed only a little more of the drink. On the last day she tried to dress for a true performance, but she was covered in her own filth, and she shook so much from the poison that she could not put on her feathered mask or the buffalo horn of the society. First she tried to sing of the Manitou's dream, but she could only weep. Then she tried to sing Running Wind's

Chapter V

song of all living things, but she could not hum with her own pulse. About midday she fell on the frozen ground twitching. When her body was still we found she had choked upon her tongue. We washed her and placed her on a platform, but there was no one with a bone whistle, and the trader went away with all her furs."

All that long month of silence the band mourned for something more than the life of Dancing Light. Peewit went about his tasks tense with the strained confusion. His grandfather seemed withered as he sat day after day upon a high hill. It seemed to Peewit that every breeze and summer storm took away more strength and washed away the laughter. The men, including his father, had gone to try to make a treaty with the traders. At last they returned, but Peewit's father lay upon a travois and instead of twelve strong men, they were only seven frightened men.

Peewit watched his mother unwind the bandages and smelled the putrefied flesh and saw a strange black hole at his father's shoulder. He did not wait to hear the story but ran until he could wrap his grandfather in a cloak.

"My grandfather, you must come down and end your silence. My father's leg smells of rot and you must cut it, and there is a hole in his shoulder which was not made by any arrow. Of the twelve who went, only seven have returned, and unless you act now as a healer, all who listen to them talk will be infected with this disease of fear which is written on their faces."

There was no reply.

Peewit tried every argument he could think of until his throat hurt and his body ached. Running Wind sat huddled, gazing at the horizon of the mountains. At last Peewit pulled out the bone whistle and played Running Wind's song of life. But he did not begin with the pulse, he began with the sounds of cold stars and lonely darkness, and grief for all that was no more. He blew softly but the sound was all around the two of them. He played the sound of water, of green things growing, and of animals raising their snouts toward spring. He played of a man chasing a buffalo, singing songs of healing on behalf of others, and playing with his children before nightfall. Then he played of laughter and sunlight and though the man and his children would die there would be new life again, and grieving would be part of it, but beneath all would be the laughter of life. Peewit did not look at Running Wind when finally the whistle fell against his chest. He looked at his hands and knew he could do no more.

"You are right my Peewit and I have been wrong. Lend me your shoulder and we return to camp." Running Wind grasped the young boy and Peewit stumbled often in the long walk back.

When Running Wind had cut away the rotting leg, and Peewit had gently sought in the shoulder wound until he brought out a metal ball, Peewit's mother bound the wounds and the camp assembled to sing the healing. By the first frosts, his father's fevers had ended and his shoulder was no longer draining. This time the band moved into the foothills for the winter, camping in a deep cleft where the winds could not find them easily. How small the band was Peewit thought one clear night as he came down the hills from his snares.

"Men should not have to hide from other men," he thought. He wondered what chant he would learn this night. It seemed every moment of this winter was filled with lessons and now it was not he who asked the questions.

Chapter V

Spring came and they emerged from the cleft of the hills and three other bands waited to welcome them to the plains. Peewit's sister was married and the whiskers of the crocus faded as the earth grew warm again. One evening, as Running Wind and Peewit worked together on his father's withered arm, he bade them stop. When he spoke he did not look at his son, but at Running Wind.

"Peewit must leave us. It is time for his own quest to become a man, and we have delayed him too long because he has become Fix-it Find-it to all of us. But now my father, you are old and I am maimed. We see the bands shrinking each day. Perhaps Peewit will not return, and perhaps he will not see visions, but in my heart I feel our only hope is to send him. We have trusted young men in the past to learn what would be needed for their own time. It is Peewit's turn to go and seek for answers."

Running Wind let his tears fall and as the white hair blew across his face he smiled at Peewit. "I fear I shall be gone to the wind before you return, but you already have my heart within your heart."

"Why can I not go to a close and sacred hill as my brothers did? Then I would be with you all in a moon's passing."

Running Wind looked west across the mountains and his father spoke.

"You have had two names; one, Fix-it Find-it began as a name of scorn. Now that name calls forth our hope, for you have truly become a watcher. If there is a way to fix this sickness, then I believe you are the one who may find it. I do not know if you can find it on any sacred hill. But as your father, as a member of the medicine society, and as a 'healer with words' as once you called me, I charge you to seek it as far as you must until you know truly it is found."

"You do not charge me to find my own guardian spirit?"

"Peewit, pay attention. We have given you our teachings, but now we know we must have new teachings to strengthen what we know. As the seasons change, so man changes, and we need to learn new ways. Now I tell you as your Grandfather, and also as Running Wind, and as the singer of the Medicine Society, you must seek more than a guardian for your own spirit. You must seek for us all, the teachings which will bring peace and wholeness to every spirit which is lost. Not only the Cree but even for the traders of poison and the people who will come following them."

"I am only one boy," said Peewit, and his hand clasped the bone whistle. "I do not want to leave you."

Chapter VI

Chapter VI

When he was a very old man telling the story of his great journey to his own grandson, Peewit's voice would fail when he tried to speak of the parting. Always, he would sing of the loneliness of the Manitou's dream when he spoke of the first days of walking toward the mountains.

Then he would describe how his fingers would trace the shape of his father's obsidian knife, tied to his thigh. He would clasp his whistle and think of Low Horn and Loneseer and Morning Cloud and Dancing Light. He held his little pouch of herbs to his nostrils hoping to gain strength from the medicines placed there by his mother. When he was sitting, tired of walking, he would pull from another pouch Running Wind's cup with which he had danced. His fingers by themselves would find the grooves where Running Wind had held it. Each time he drank from it, he felt the warmth of his Grandfather's skin. In the night he could hear the soft rising chuckle and see the bright hawk look of waiting and feel the last touch of white hair blowing as the old man turned away when they had said farewell.

Each time he reached the crest of a new line of hills, Peewit made his little camp and watched, marking within his mind the map he saw in each direction. He noted that the higher he climbed the more the plants and birds changed, and the more hungry he became each day. He chanted his observations into song, making sure that each new thing was added to the song. Sometimes he sat and watched through the night and slept in the warmth of the day. He was glad it was summer for the mountains were cold. When he first heard the growl of an avalanche, he wondered if his sister was right after all, that guardian spirits were terrors. But the sound came again, and Peewit's curiosity led him onward. He watched the destruction of the ice and felt the weight of it thunder against the earth, and looked for evidence that there had been other avalanches in other spring times.

The lambs of the mountain sheep played in the meadows where he watched. Everywhere there were birds he had not known before, each to be understood. He tried to relate the new encounters to something on the plains. As time passed he had explored the snow line, been bruised against rocks in a waterfall, and found a pass downward, he knew it was nearly summer. Here there were no wide plains as he had expected, but instead even more mountains to the west. The narrow valleys were richer in animals than any Peewit had seen. Surely there must be a tribe, feasting on all this plenty. He kept moving south and west, hoping that soon he would find an answer.

By autumn he had met two tribes. Each was startled but fed the boy and cheered when he joined their young men to dance, especially the Chicken dance. Each place, Peewit listened and tried to learn the language as his father had taught him, and from each tribe he learned about the new plants. He could see in their eyes that these were happy people, without the sickness of fear, and he heard nothing about poisoned water brought by strangers.

Chapter VI

He spent his first winter with the Nez Perce who lived together on a high plateau and taught him new songs to the earth. By spring he could speak comfortably with their old men, and with the herbalists who enjoyed his company. He was shy among the young people and did not gamble with them, and they in turn were shy of one who had come so far alone on his quest. These bands lived in harmony and expected to always, so Peewit knew he must move on.

Every evening alone he would practice his songs and repeat his maps. Sometimes he would take out the cup and try to make it dance, but those were lonely nights, full of memories and longing. He crossed a river and joined a group of young men working their way north along its bank. They laughed at his ignorance of their spear fishing but were proud that he learned quickly from them. They taught him bark weaving and showed him how to make cloaks against the rain and mists from the river.

When they reached camp, Peewit was astonished by its size and thought he must have come in time for a great festival. But it was not so. He grew homesick as he inspected the smoking lodges with their rows of fish. This strange tribe was only familiar with the banks along the huge river and they were astonished when he said he must go onward across the mountains to the west. They kept him awake nights with stories of the demons and dangers of the mountains, and in the days they fed him so much that he longed for his solitude. When he left they told him they would sing their songs for the dead, for any who left their river would surely die.

High in the next range of mountains, Peewit built a sweat lodge and fasted and rubbed his body with sweet grasses. Would he never be free of the smell of fish? He thought of other wanderers for whom every place was a home, to be sung about once seen. These fisher folk were certainly in harmony with their river and valley, but their world was small, the horizons high and narrow, and the sky above a stormy one. If change came to these people, what would happen to them? If they had to flee from the river, would they still know who they were? Was this part of his quest?

Peewit sang and looked eastward across so many mountains. Fear was such a strange thing. He had found people who shared their food eagerly, but who were afraid of being in a different place upon the earth. He had met tribes who would never share their food, but who had no fear of wandering the land. Their fear was of those who might take away their food. So, what was the answer? If you had plenty of food, you did not fear it might be taken, as if you had much space, you did not fear to move in it? Did that mean whatever you did not have you feared? Peewit sang to Running Wind, asking his questions, while at the same time part of him wondered if somewhere the old man's body lay upon a platform for the winds.

He played on his bone whistle and played the memories of Loneseer and Running Wind laughing together. That night his dreams were filled with memories of the first time he joined them in the sacred lodge. He awakened tired, having dreamt of Dancing Light. A jay adopted him that morning, chatting and begging along the trail. Peewit complained to the bird and felt better after it had scolded him soundly.

How old were these mountains, Peewit wondered. He remembered from times in the coal country that there were leaves and shells impressed within the stones. How long did that take? He had crumbled the stones from his own rivers into sand when he was just a child, and knew that some stones could be cut to shape other stones. He puzzled over his father's obsidian blade, and remembered that

Chapter VI

the Nez Perce had tiny arrowheads for hunting birds which were made from the same hard material. These mountains were different, sharper, like spears instead of hills. He seemed always to be in a cloud, cut off from both the sky and the valleys below.

He wore a cloak like the fisher folk but he seemed always to be wet. At last he had to rest and as he searched for shelter he was surprised. The streams were rushing to the west, but the clouds were pushing east. What was the smell in the clouds? Something new and unknown? In the morning, in the mist, Peewit followed the stream downward. He was so used to the mist that he almost fell against a totem pole. He realized that there was within the mist the smell of wood smoke and a camp nearby. Then he examined the carving.

"It looks like a greeting song made in wood," he thought and sat to make a memory of it from the top to the bottom and back again. Peewit did not know how tall he had grown in his trek, so it was good that the little coastal people found him seated. They thought he was praying before their totem pole. Their language was stranger than anything he had heard so far; the fish smell was even stronger. They gestured for him to follow and were astonished by his height and the hide leggings he had outgrown. By this time in his travels, Peewit had learned to guard his face, so they did not see that he was equally astonished by them, their huge canoes and their houses on stilts.

Over the next months he would come to love these people, recognizing their reverence as they carved. Long before he had learned their language, he knew that their greeting songs made things new again. On the fourth day of his stay, Peewit had his vision.

After they had carefully examined Peewit, the Haida gave him a tour of the village, watching his gestures, understanding his attention, and pleased by his curiosity. They could feel the anguish inside him of all the questions he wanted to ask, and two of the old women talked to him constantly and grieved that he did not understand. He sang a greeting song to the rain, and they were pleased and then they then sang a song to great waters. A bed in one of the houses was made for him. By the second day he knew this was the home of the healer; and Peewit shared that he came from healer's family. He was told by his host that he was welcome to become a member of this healer's family.

There were herbs drying in the house, and safely hung bundles ready for use. That night his dreams were of the Arapaho woman who had learned his language while she waited for her husband to die. The coastal people accepted Peewit's constant repetition of their sounds and his mimicry of everything he heard. As they were harvesting from a garden plot, a cry came from the mists along the stream.

At once they were all running, down the river bank. Peewit was pulled into one of the great canoes as it was pushed into water. He crouched and clung to the floor of the canoe out of the way of all the strange activity. The speed was beyond anything he had known, far faster than a frightened horse. He saw above him that the mist was thinning. All eight men were paddling as fast as they could, and Peewit watched their skill with awe. Suddenly they were in brilliant sunshine, and there were huge flights of birds above them. The men put up their paddles laughing, and gestured that he should kneel beside them so that he could see. When he was kneeling in the prow, he looked up into his vision.

At first, he felt blinded. This was the true dancing light of the Manitou's dream, and Peewit laughed that he had come into it. The members of the Haida tribe laughed with him and pointed. Peewit

Chapter VI

did not see what they were seeing. There was sky, and a bird, the sun was still the sun, but there was no land. The canoe was riding only water and the mist above the water was taking the light of the sun and seemed to be changing it, giving new light back. As far as he could see there was no horizon, the water became the sky, and the sky became the water, and all he felt was joy. The men were pointing, urgently, Peewit followed their gestures.

There, riding the waters with them, were many giant fish. Bigger than buffalo and seeming to remain still while only the waters moved. Across the water came the low greeting song of the whales. The Haida listened, silent with delight.

Peewit listened and heard a song he had heard before. The whales changed their notes, higher, welcoming. Peewit pulled out the bone whistle and answered the song. Back and forth, back and forth, and all of Peewit poured into the bone. The great whales answered him, he knew it. At last the waters were restless as the whales stopped singing and the men turned their canoes. When they reached the inlet, Peewit understood why the village perched away from the sea. He realized he had come to the end of the earth at last, and that this must be the water of the Manitou's dream.

As soon as they landed and Peewit helped pull the canoe high up on the banks, the people gathered to touch the bone whistle. When he would not play again, they understood that it was sacred to him. Now he was not a fool without language, and everyday brought changes. When finally he could ask his questions, Peewit wanted to know why the village was not nearer the water. He was always eager to go down to the inlet, but the people approached it with a kind of fear. They were patient with him and drew pictures of great waves and faces of anger. Peewit did not understand until the old woman

The Shaman's Child

healer said she would show him.

She loaded him with a heavy pack and they set off on a trail, climbing for hours. When they descended to a rocky beach in a small cove, Peewit was puzzled when the woman made camp on the highest, most uncomfortable part of the beach. He explored, turning over shells, watching crabs and finding skeletons of creatures he had never imagined. The seaweed intrigued him and the smell of life from the sea brought his laughter bubbling. The old woman watched him tolerantly until their meal was ready. At dusk, she made Peewit sit on a bed of boughs and drew a sacred barrier around him. He understood he was to stay in place. He would rather have walked and explored, but she was kind so he must obey. She settled easily on to her own bed of boughs and sang to him of the raven and the bear and their cleverness in surviving within their world.

The mists hid the waters, but Peewit listened, breathing deeply because he was so close. He slept, tossed, and then was suddenly awake. The sea was close to him and covered the entire beach where he had walked. It was almost to their beds. He did not move from the sacred circle. The old woman talked, but he did not understand all that she was trying to teach. Again he slept, but wakened in the warm dawn. The waters were gone; once again there was a beach. The old woman removed the sacred circle and Peewit ran down to the water. There were new shells, new runnels, new skeletons and different sea plants. He tried to make sense of the mystery but the woman sent him off to gather wood.

All day she kept him busy. When the sea rose again, they watched it come and he paced it, trying to see and understand. This time, when the sea drew back, he walked with it and stood on the slippery stones, feeling the sucking power within the water. The old woman

Chapter VI

called urgently, so Peewit helped her remove their packs up the bank into the shelter of the woods. There was a wind, so the woman wove them capes from the boughs, and Peewit tried to imitate her deft skills. She kept glancing at the water.

When the storm came, Peewit watched the power and thunder of the waves and felt the spray against him. The old woman asked had he understood the power of the waters which forever went back and forth. She told him that was why they had to live high above the inlet, for none could say when the waves would reach them. Now he had a new mystery to watch.

Autumn came and Peewit helped the band prepare for the cold, but each day he tried to slip away to watch the sea. He learned to paddle in the great canoes, and how to make and cast the fish nets. He learned to listen in the night for the sea to tell him what the weather would be. There was laughter in the seals and in the huge flocks of birds going south, and in the people as they sought among the great trees for their carving poles.

Alone sometimes, Peewit would sing of his home, and in his mind he could see the rolling plains and the white hair of Loneseer and Running Wind. All through the winter he saw great mountains of ice move slowly through the water. He watched the ebb and flow and knew that it was somehow connected to the ebbing of the moon. He was fascinated by all that was tossed to the shore by the sea. The Haida showed him their collection of strange things, and walked with him in the skeleton of a great whale. The small sound of the bone whistle was plaintive for Peewit, and he often felt wistful when the people danced and feasted.

One of the oldest men of the village enjoyed Peewit's curiosity and

The Shaman's Child

let him watch him carving during the winter days. There were songs and tales of the wild things and the tricks and pranks they played. Although the Haida mistrusted weather and feared forests, they sang of nature's power with admiration, not fear. As the weather began to change, and even before the sky was filled again with birds Peewit smelled the warmth coming. He went to the cove late one afternoon and settled where once the old healer had drawn a sacred circle for him. He watched the glitter on the water and played his bone whistle.

He played Running Wind's song of living things, but now with his own story and experience as parts of the song. The sun's evening pathway led to his feet, and the whales, moving north, called out to him. Even in the darkness they sang. The moon rose new above him and the water came gently up to Peewit, washed him, and ebbed softly away. In the grey morning when there was neither sky nor sea, Peewit knew that it would always be so. Here at last was healing. As the stones bore the images of the ferns of long ago, so the sea and the sun would bring forth living things long after his songs had been forgotten. Peewit brought out the cup he had carried so long and instead of a feather, danced with the obsidian knife and sang the song of living things. When he fell asleep in the cove, the water returned and told him it was time to go.

The Haida offered him a house and a girl to marry and even a great canoe, but he refused their adoption. The healing woman gave him fresh herbs for his long walk, and the old carver gave him a long parcel wrapped tightly and told him he must open it only once he had crossed the mountains. His friends walked with him on the first morning toward the dawn, but they were afraid, so he sung them safely home and climbed alone.

Chapter VII

Chapter VII

His pace was fast and strong until he realized he might not see the sea again. Should he turn back? No, he could not. But he found the tallest tree and climbed. There was the glittering ribbon amidst the mist, the beginning and the ending of the horizon. He breathed the salt taste and felt the pull of the sea again, but he climbed down and turned east.

This time Peewit did not follow the great river south and did not retrace his route to the Nez Perce. He travelled without lingering, pushed by a strange sense of urgency. He discovered the Kootenay people and they understood when he spoke. They had news of a new tribe over the mountains. It was now late autumn, too cold to go high against the ice. The Kootenay hunters told him there was a pass where warm waters bubbled up from the stones and a man could move from one such pool to another without fear of freezing. They dressed him in warm skins and told him he must rub his skin with fat each night after he found the hot springs. Their memories were accurate the route was easier than Peewit imagined. When he wakened one morning after a blizzard, the sun was on his face. He must have crossed the highest point. After a few more hours of walking he checked, the streams were running east.

The Shaman's Child

With the knowledge that he was nearing the plains, he was suddenly weak and sat down panting. As his hand fell to his side it brushed the rough bark of the carver's gift. Slowly Peewit undid the bark. The carver had made him another bone whistle, but this one was as long as his arm. The holes were placed just as they were in his own small flute. Peewit remembered that he himself had walked within the skeleton of a whale, where this bone must have been found. The whales had given this flute.

He sucked upon his cold lips until they were soft and warm, and then he blew. Wonder, upon wonder, the sound was a memory of the whales' song. Not as deep because he was not playing it with echoes from the water. The sound was large and captured the song made by the unity of sea and sky. In awe, Peewit held the bone flute away from him. This was not a whistle to be played on the platforms for the dead. This was a true medicine flute to play the songs of dreams, and to play away the lostness from fearful eyes. He wrapped it again but this time, hung it against his skin, and against the small flute from Low Horn.

All the way down into the plains, Peewit rehearsed his new song. Over and over he tried to catch the ebb and flow the sea as a comfort. He tried to sing a song which said that even if his band disappeared, life would still sing its song. The winds around him reminded him that he had no idea where he was going and who, of those he loved, might still be alive.

In the clefts of the foothills he found no winter camps. He followed the river toward the coal country. At night he sheltered on the banks among the willows. He arrived into the familiar valley on a day when even his eyes ached with cold. He smelled smoke and called out a greeting again and again. It was very odd; there was just one

Chapter VII

tattered tent, no hobbled horses, and no sign of the band. He stood outside and called and told all who dwelt there that he was a child of the medicine society returned from his quest.

He heard a woman's voice. "Fix-it Find-it, is it you?"

"Arapaho woman, wife of Low Horn, are you returned to my people?"

Peewit stared at the old face, shocked by how withered she was. He entered the shelter as her hands grasped him. She was too weak to stand. The stench stunned him. He sat on his heels trying to breathe.

"Why do you have the dead within your teepee?"

"I am not strong enough to move him."

Peewit carried her to shelter against the bank and then drew the corpse out on its boughs. He gathered brushwood and coal, but did not try to build a platform. He lit the fire and emptied the tent of everything that would burn. It took him most of the day to find conifers and bring back the boughs and return the old woman to a fresh bed.

The pyre had burned low and Peewit sang a blessing over the embers. Peewit knew the woman was sick, but this was a strange illness. At least she knew him; she might know where his people had gone.

It took many days and nights before Peewit could sort through her words to make the tale. Low Horn's widow was Quiet Rain; her voice vanished even as she spoke. The Arapaho had fled into the Blackfoot lands but the traders for furs had brought with them this sickness. Many who caught it were dead or blind. Peewit's own mother was now blind. When the strange disease came to the Blackfeet, the Arapaho had fled north to ask the medicine people for help. Sickness found them all first, and now the medicine bands were far away to somewhere she did not know, a sacred valley they had called it.

None who had the sickness could make the journey, and they were burning all the contaminated belongings behind them. She had the first signs, the red rash, and so she had been left, and Peewit had just burned the remains of the leader of the medicine society who had died of the sickness. No, not his grandfather, but the old man who conducted the ceremonies.

"Who leads the band?"

"Your father," she whispered.

The rest of that lonely winter, Peewit thought hard. They must not move to join if there was any sickness still, or if he fell to it. So he foraged and sang and practiced with the obsidian knife and his grandfather's cup, and Quiet Rain grew strong enough to help with the cooking. She taught him Low Horn's healing songs, and the Arapaho songs and they talked of all the places he had seen. She was the first to hear the whale bone flute, but Peewit would not speak of his vision.

Early in the spring Peewit found and skinned a dead buffalo and killed a buck deer with thankful prayers. The woman made them new clothes, but Peewit insisted that she only work away from the teepee. He smoked meat for their journey. When the weather was soft enough for travel, he built two sweat houses and took Quiet rain's clothing and his own and burned everything with the old teepee. He passed everything he owned through the fire and steam in the

Chapter VII

sweat house. At last they were ready, and Peewit led her north to the valley of sweet grass.

As they journeyed he watched the lights dance in the northern sky and thought of their dance on the Ice Mountains as they floated in the great water.

"Is it a good land where the people go?"

Quiet Rain looked east back the way they had come where the earth was covered in yellow buffalo beans and the meadowlarks were singing.

"The lands are big enough for all to share, and the Manitou is in all peoples."

"Even in the traders who bring sickness and poison?"

"Yes, even so, though I do not understand that. But all living things are part of the great dream, even if we wear different moccasins."

"You are now an even stranger man than you were as a boy."

Peewit laughed and the old woman laughed and the journey became easier.

It was almost summer when they moved into the northern foothills. Peewit welcomed again the fresh smell of the mountains, and the Arapaho woman wanted every new thing explained to her.

What patience my grandfather had," thought Peewit and he wept, grieving for his beloved teacher.

The Shaman's Child

"Who are you, and why do you come near the valley of sweet grass?" a voice called down from a high cliff.

"We are Quiet Rain of the Arapaho and Peewit, Fix-it Find-it, returned from his vision quest."

"Do you bring the sickness?"

"No, and we have burned all things behind us."

Peewit did not wait for further words; he knew the child who had called was taking news back to the camp.

When they emerged on the edge of the long and lovely valley, Quiet Rain gasped at its beauty. "What is this place?"

"It is the sacred valley where we say the first medicine gathering was held when the first people were made."

"I do not see the camp."

"It is always off the side, to keep the sacred place undamaged."

Slowly they moved together down the hills. Ponies with young foals came trusting to greet them. At last they could see the camp, and Peewit was once again shy. Fix-it Find-it had returned, but would it matter?

Quiet Rain moved forward, eagerly, and a small crowd gathered at the trail's end. Was the white haired woman really his mother? Yes, she was blind, but she was embracing Quiet Rain. Who was the other woman holding a baby, and the young man beside her? Was that

Chapter VII

his older brother? How did his older brother become a small man?

And then there were no more questions, for the little crowd parted for an old man whose white hair flowed down over his shoulders, and who stood, proud of his tears, waiting. With a gasp and a cry, Peewit ran into Running Wind's arms and they laughed as they had never laughed before. Then the whole band laughed there in the valley of the sweet grass.

The Shaman's Child

Epilogue

First a sweat bath, then a feast, then like all wanderers Peewit had to hear the tales and put names to faces of all who gathered.

"But you said my father led the band?" Peewit asked Quiet Rain, but his mother answered.

"Yes, he did when we first left her, but he too sickened and died. I alone remembered the way but since I cannot see I had to talk it to others."

"And you, Loneseer's guide, who watched us when we learned from Morning Cloud, how did you come to marry my brother?"

"In all your travels did you not learn how a man and a woman marry?"

The best was for last. "My grandfather, you are stronger than when I left, and you promised me then only a long sorrow."

"Yes, Peewit and I came here to the valley as soon as you left on your journey. But I could not die. You left me your questions, for every time I tried to fast and give away my body, I would think of what you might be learning. So I stayed hidden and the few who sought peace stayed with me. Now the band is gathered, but tomorrow more will come for the traders chase hard and fast across the plains."

Peewit sighed and looked around him. Those watching him saw a tall young stranger, weathered and muscled. His eyes were gentler even than the eyes of Running Wind, and they were fixed beyond everything he saw. He was still intent, and there were shadows of the boy upon the man, but no one who saw him now would send him on a mere errand.

"You are tired, my son, and it is a mother's choice to send you to bed, even if it be the last time I can do so."

Peewit slept very soundly, the bone whistle and the whale flute beside him. Running Wind listened to him breathe and from time to time reached out and touched the young body. Each time he did so Peewit would smile, and the sight of that smile was better than sleep for Running Wind.

Soon it was the equinox, and Running Wind stood before the assembly at the great festival. They did not build a sacred lodge within the sacred valley, but named it once more and told the stories of the first things. There were so few gathered there was no need for rules. Running Wind was the only leader left. Morning Cloud sang and Peewit's mother and a man from the east called Blue Hills.

They played the hand games together and were silent. Running Wind told the story of a boy called Fix-it Find-it who was given a bone whistle and who learned the ways of all that he saw, but who was still mocked as the boy who did not see visions. And now this boy stood before them to tell them of his vision, so that he too would

Epilogue

be initiated as a healer, a maker of things new once more.

For the first time, Peewit stood alone before the tribe and began to sing. He did not sing of his journey, but began with the story of Low Horn's death platform and the sound of the whistle as it taught him of dying, of discarding what was not useful or real any longer. He sang then of the treaty journeys and the words making peace, bringing harmony among the bands. He sang of Loneseer and his healing hands and the terrible loneliness of a healer without an apprentice.

At last he began the tale of his travels, first using the bone whistle and dancing to show them how the mountain sheep played. He sang of welcome feasts given by strangers and his questions about the age of the stones. He told how he came down from the mists to the edge of the world where the Manitou's waters met the sky and the light danced and even the great fish sang of the Manitou's dream.

He picked up the whale bone flute and played his whale song. It was a song of no horizons, of Ice Mountains driven by the waters, and clouds of birds above, shimmering as they flew. When he put down the flute, the tribe was still, and Peewit began to hum. He did not hum with a drum, or to his pulse, he hummed of the ebb and flow of the waters. When the people swayed with that rhythm he sang again, of what strange things the oceans brought to the shore. He sang of the moon pulling on the waters, and the great tide which the year before had come and bathed him and gone back again.

His voice was full of joy when he sang that all of the wandering peoples might one day die, and the buffalo might vanish, and even the poison of the traders would be forgotten, as would the peoples who carved trees into animals. But he sang that none of this change, and none of the grief they felt, and none of their own sickness would ever change the ebb and flow of the waters. As long as the sun made a pathway on the waves to every watcher, there would be something living, something laughing with the joy of the Manitou's great dream. He did not sing any more but picked up the cup of Running Wind and the obsidian knife, and without a shadow, taught them to dance together the dance of life.

So Peewit became a shaman. Running Wind died after one more winter. Peewit led the tribe north to join the Chipewyan far from the traders on the plains. Until he was a very old man and could not even travel with a travois, whenever he was called out to sing a healing song, or tell of the waters without horizon, he would take his bone whistle and his whale bone flute and go to serve. Long after he died, those who had heard him told the story of the boy who did not see visions who became the singer of what is real.

Author's Biography

Heather Wood Ion is a chief executive and cultural anthropologist who specializes in turning around troubled organizations. Her first book, *Third-Class Ticket*, has been translated into Italian, Hindi, Japanese and Chinese and is currently being made into a feature film.

Another book, with Saul Levine M.D., *Against Terrible Odds*, applies her knowledge of social and cultural recovery to the profound issues of individual resilience.

Making Doctors provides the biographies of a father and daughter who each became a great physician, and traces the history of their work from a sod hut on the prairie to the present day.

The Shaman's Child

Made in the USA
Charleston, SC
14 July 2014